THE BIG CAT MYSTERY

THE TED WILFORD SERIES

THE BIG CAT MYSTERY

NORVIN PALLAS

yh

WILDSIDE PRESS

To Linda, Kathleen, and Anne

CHAPTER 1

OFF TO VANISHING LAKE

"Yes, Mr. Jackson, I can hear you all right, except for that one word. I'm not sure I caught it correctly. Will you spell it for me, please? . . . L–E–O–P–A–R–D. Yes, I have it now. Well, I'll probably send a man up to Vanishing Lake to check into it. Thank you for calling, Mr. Jackson."

Ted Wilford, busy at his desk in the office of the Forestdale *Town Crier*, where he worked during college vacations, had not stopped typing when the phone first rang. It rang so frequently that if he and Mr. Dobson and Miss Monroe and Carl Allison all stopped their work for every call, the newspaper would probably have come out on Wednesdays and Saturdays, instead of Tuesdays and Fridays.

But Ted's desk was close to that of the editor, and at the first indication that Mr. Dobson was having trouble hearing his caller, he stopped typing. Then as he caught the spelled-out word he was immediately all attention. A leopard—in or around the camp at Vanishing Lake? How could that be? And if Mr. Dobson was promising to send up a man, whom could he send? Besides Ted himself, there was only Carl, the newspaper's regular reporter, who had not only a full schedule of assignments, but also a strong distaste for "foolishness." Under this heading came any sort of assignment that seemed of doubtful benefit to the newspaper. Though he always went if Mr. Dobson told him to, he did it with poor grace and often failed to follow the story up.

Ted's approach was quite different. He figured that Mr. Dobson was the editor and must decide whether a story had possibilities or not. Furthermore, although he had no objection to typing up stories and to the thousand and one other routine tasks around a newspaper office, Ted was always glad of the opportunity to break away from his desk on an elusive but potentially big story. He was really more of an office boy than a reporter, but that didn't alter the fact that he *hoped* to be a reporter someday. His elder brother, Ronald, now a reporter on a metropolitan paper, had set the example for him.

So Ted anticipated an interesting assignment even before Mr. Dobson hung up the receiver and turned to him.

"Ted, that call was from a man named George Jackson up at Vanishing Lake. He tells me there are rumors of a leopard running around in the woods up there. Footprints have been found, and several of the guests claim to have caught a glimpse of the animal slinking through the woods. Obviously I can't spare Carl for what may prove a wild-goose chase. But I wonder if you'd like to take a run up there?"

"When do I start?" asked Ted eagerly.

The editor nodded approvingly. "That's the spirit. Of course you realize it could easily be a false alarm. On the other hand, it might be true, and might not only lead to a good story, but may even be dangerous. I'm counting on you to use your own good sense, Ted. Don't believe unsubstantiated stories, don't fall for a prank, and on the other hand, don't endanger yourself unnecessarily. Otherwise you're on your own. You can follow the story as far as you think necessary."

"Is Mr. Jackson the owner of the resort, or is he one of our correspondents?"

"Neither, Ted. I've never heard of him before, but I believe he is a guest. As for his reliability, you'll have to judge that for yourself. I can only say he didn't sound particularly excited or hysterical over the phone, the way some people might have."

"How did he happen to call the *Town Crier?* Vanishing Lake is quite a way from here."

"I suppose he's one of our readers, and it's natural to call a paper you're familiar with when something like this comes up."

But Ted was thinking that the *Town Crier*, in spite of its small size, had a reputation for reliability. Mr. Dobson was an influential person, and there were a good many important people who would listen to him. Perhaps it was merely his loyalty to the *Town Crier*, but Ted felt no doubt about why Mr. Jackson had called this paper, instead of one of those closer to the resort.

"One more thing, Ted," the editor went on, "if you were a full-time employee here you would surely be entitled to a vacation. Though you've only worked on a part-time basis, you've helped us a number of times when we've been pinched, and I feel I owe you something. So I want you to have some fun while you're up at the lake. Do you care for fishing? I understand it's very good there."

"No, I'm not fond of fishing, but I'd like a chance to improve my tennis game."

"Excellent. Suppose I reserve a cottage for a week. Then, if the story doesn't pan out, you can still have some fun. Do you think Nelson would be interested?"

"Interested in a vacation for a week? I should say so. We were planning some sort of vacation, but hadn't made up our minds. I'd better call him, though."

"Then I'll make the reservations. And when I'm calling I'll find out if there really is a guest named George Jackson registered there. That'll give us a little something to start out on."

Ted and his friend Nelson Morgan were on their way to Vanishing Lake soon after the lunch hour. Nelson had his camera securely packed with the rest of his luggage, and had hopes of making some pictures that might eventually be published. His camera, his car, and his services had been useful to the newspaper in the past, and he was glad that Mr. Dobson appreciated them. And while the *Town Crier* never used very many pictures, and could not afford to pay much, Nelson had his own dream.

"A picture of a posse rounding up a wild leopard in the woods— why, the wire services ought to gobble that right up. I might find myself famous overnight. Only one thing wrong with it"—and his exuberant tone sobered—"there isn't any leopard."

"How do you know that?" asked Ted cautiously.

"Oh, come on, Ted, can't you *smell?* A story like that has an odor to it like a cheese factory. Mr. Dobson's got a reputation for shrewdness, and he must have smelled it, too. He just saw a chance to give us a free vacation and pay off a debt he thinks he owes us—even though he's already paid us in cash."

"Don't underestimate Mr. Dobson. He's got a devious mind, and he might have been thinking of both things at once. There just might be a story here, so why not follow it up and see where it leads, if we can? I know it doesn't sound very probable, but there *could* be a leopard. Unlikely things happen every day. That's how newspapers stay in business."

Nelson was silent until he maneuvered his car around a snaky curve. "All right, Ted, what have you got to go on? You've had a telephone call from a man you never heard of before, and he claims a few tracks have been found and some strange animal has been sighted in the woods. Listen, if your paper printed a story that a pink elephant with pearly wings and wearing roller skates was roaming around, within a week you'd be able to round up a dozen witnesses who'd claim they saw it. Maybe they're crazy, maybe they just want their names in the paper, but maybe they're like a lot of people who aren't sure just what they did see."

"Oh, I admit that we don't have very much proof that there *is* a leopard. I just wondered what proof you had that there *isn't*."

"All right, where did it come from? Leopards don't grow on bushes, you know."

"It could have escaped from a circus or a zoo."

"Sure it could. And don't you think the police and the officials would be straining their backs trying to find it? And how can you keep something like that a secret very long?"

"They might for a while. Maybe it wasn't even reported to the police, or maybe the police are trying not to alarm the public. Anyway, judging by that phone call, they *haven't* kept it secret."

"They wouldn't even try. Oh, I agree, that if they weren't sure a leopard had escaped, they might try to cover it up until they knew. But if they did know a leopard was running around loose they'd have to warn the public."

"Well"—Ted was forced to agree reluctantly, but sought some other argument—"it doesn't have to be a leopard. It might be a big lynx, or a wild dog, or maybe a cougar."

"O.K. Now what's this animal eating, this animal that's big enough to be mistaken for a leopard? I know there are woods around the lake, but they're not as big as a jungle. How far do you suppose a leopard wanders every day for its food—five miles, ten, or fifteen? Well, then, how could it avoid being seen for very long?"

"That's exactly the point—it *has* been seen."

"*Maybe* it has. You won't know for sure until you get some better reports than that one telephone call. What about food? I don't know what a leopard might catch in those woods—a few rabbits, squirrels, chipmunks, or wild rats. Would that be enough for a leopard?"

"I don't really know. There've been deer reported in the woods up that way."

"Sure, there're *always* deer reported when the resorts are trying to attract hunters, but I never knew anybody who found any."

"If the leopard had only escaped a few days ago, hunger might not be a serious problem so far. But if it is getting hungry by now— good and ravenously hungry—then it might become a real threat. That's all the more reason why we can't write this off as just another yarn."

"Oh, all right, Ted, I don't need any arguments to convince me we ought to take a nice week's vacation. I wonder how Vanishing Lake got its name?"

"I've heard two different stories about it. One story is that it refers to a vanishing tribe of Indians. The other version is that an early explorer set it down on his map, then when he returned a few years later he was unable to find it, so he called it Vanishing Lake. Maybe it really did disappear. I suppose a couple of years of drought might do it, and of course the dam at the end of it hadn't been built then."

"More likely he was just a poor map maker."

"Whatever it was, it makes a good name for a vacation resort," Ted remarked, consulting a map to see how close they were to their destination.

"Well, what's our program, after we get to the camp?" Nelson asked.

"Look up George Jackson first thing, I suppose."

"That's another thing, Ted—doesn't that name sound phony?"

"Why should it? There are lots of people named George, and lots of people named Jackson, so why not George Jackson?"

"Because it sounds too simple—like John Smith."

"And if he had a name twenty-six letters long, you'd think that was phony, too, wouldn't you?"

"I suppose so." Nelson grunted. "Say, how dangerous is a leopard, anyway?"

"I thought you were convinced there isn't any leopard," Ted joked.

"I am, but I believe in being careful."

"I've heard that some hunters consider it the most dangerous animal of all. It's smaller than a lion, but still big enough, and more treacherous and less predictable. I imagine it's a better climber, too, so that gives it a third dimension."

"A climber, heh?" said Nelson thoughtfully.

"Oh, I wouldn't worry about it. I don't think cats are really good climbers—not in the same class with squirrels and monkeys."

"No, but they're probably as good as *I* am, and that's what's bothering me. If you can't outrun it or outclimb it or outfight it, what are you going to do?"

"Maybe there'll be some water around so you can try out-swimming it."

"That's a thought. Say, is that Vanishing Lake up ahead?"

Ted caught the sparkle of sunlight upon water. "Looks like it."

"Well, then, there's your lake, and there's your resort, and you'll soon find your Mr. Jackson. But where's your leopard? Vanished."

CHAPTER 2

MR. ARMAND'S OPINION

They drove into the resort's parking lot, got out, and Nelson locked the car. Then they paused to look around.

The lake was, of course, the center of attraction. The day had grown warm, and it looked unusually clear, cool, and enticing. A dozen people, mostly children, were scattered along the water's edge. Empty rowboats bobbed beside a small pier, while out on the water other boats were occupied by fishermen. There was even a sailboat visible, though the lake was really too small for sailing. Two long arms branched off the lake at the other end, and were concealed among the trees which came down to the edge of the water. One arm was simply a quiet backwater, but the other led to the dam. Between them was an area called The Point, which was used as a picnic grounds.

On their own side, there was a sandy beach and behind the beach were three long rows of cottages. Closest to them, a building a little larger than the rest appeared to be the business office.

"I suppose we ought to register, before we get thrown out as trespassers," Nelson commented, then added hopefully, "and then maybe a swim?"

Ted shook his head regretfully. "Business first. You ever hear about deadlines?"

"What's your deadline on this story?"

"Before any other paper gets it—if I can do it."

"And if there's a story. But there really is a story, isn't there, Ted? I mean, there doesn't have to be a leopard. Just the fact that people are all excited about something, even if it isn't true, makes a story, doesn't it?"

"Maybe, but it's not the sort of story Mr. Dobson would use. Anyway, we're a long way from Forestdale, and it would have to be a pretty big story, and have some kind of local tie-in, before it would interest a community newspaper."

Nelson stared slowly and speculatively about him. "Sure a lot of nice woods around. I wonder how big they are? Back home I didn't think they'd be large enough to hide a leopard for long, but now I'm not so sure. I did notice something, though. Except for that private gravel road we came up on, I don't think there are any other roads around."

"Unless you want to count that mud track running around this end of the lake."

"Oh, I imagine that doesn't go anywhere. It's just to take picnickers and hikers to the other side of the lake, in case they don't want to row. . . . Well, let's register, and then we'll know where we're supposed to stow our gear. I'd like to get one of the cottages in the front row, looking out on the lake, wouldn't you?"

"Don't count on it. Those are probably reserved for the long-term residents. We've only got a week, remember? We'll probably get the back row."

Ted proved to be entirely correct; they were given the very last cottage in the back row. The manager of the resort, Mr. Armand, who was presiding at the registration desk, did not surrender their keys at once. After they had each signed the register, he looked the book over carefully, then said:

"I suppose you have some identification on you?"

"My driver's license?" Nelson suggested.

"No, not your license. I meant some proof that you are working for the *Town Crier*." He didn't act suspicious of them, nor did he make any slighting remarks about their youth. His manner was quite formal, as though this were the way things ought to be done, and therefore this was the way he was doing them. The manager of a vacation resort ought to adopt a somewhat more cordial attitude than that toward his guests, Ted thought, and decided that Mr. Armand wasn't the owner, but probably a mere straw boss.

"My press card." Ted extended it for Mr. Armand to read. The manager examined it carefully before snapping the wallet shut and returning it to Ted.

"I suppose it's all right," he said grudgingly, "though these things are easily forged." He tossed the keys across the desk to them.

"There's no way I can keep you out, as long as you are well behaved and your credit remains good. But I suppose you'll do your best to pick up every rumor you can find, and maybe a few you've made up, and throw all this garbage together into a sensational front-page story. You have to get your story, don't you, to justify your swindle sheet?"

"Mr. Dobson doesn't work on that basis," said Ted evenly. "If there isn't any leopard, my paper won't print a story about it."

"Maybe you'll wish it would," said Nelson, still stung by Mr. Armand's attitude. "It might help clear up the rumors."

"Oh." The manager seemed somewhat mollified. "I'm glad you're going to treat this on a responsible basis. But of course if you're here to find out about a leopard, you are wasting both your time and your money, for naturally there isn't any leopard."

"Then where are these rumors coming from?" asked Ted.

"I can tell you exactly where they're coming from. They're being spread by Mr. George Jackson. He's a busybody of an old man who claims he discovered some tracks in the mud somewhere across the lake. Well, maybe he did, I don't know. Surely a less reliable man I've never met. But tracks don't mean a leopard."

"Something must have made the tracks," Nelson observed.

"Did you go over to look at them?" Ted questioned.

"I haven't had a chance. He only reported it this morning, and I've not been able to leave the desk. Our full staff hasn't yet arrived and we're shorthanded. But I did ask Mr. Jackson to keep the matter quiet until I could investigate. Then the old reprobate calls up the newspaper! I didn't know about it until Mr. Dobson phoned to make your reservations, but I spoke to Mr. Jackson about it afterward, and he admitted it. You can imagine how hard it was not to tell him exactly what I thought of him, but I have to remember my position here."

"He said he had witnesses," Ted pointed out.

"Maybe he does. I wouldn't know about that. But believe me, there won't be any trouble finding witnesses now. You boys ever study psychology? They've got one test where they hand the subject a completely blank paper, and later a lot of people claim they saw something on it."

"Why do you suppose Mr. Jackson is doing this?"

"Who knows? Maybe he really believes it. Or maybe he's looking for excitement, and wants to be important. Maybe he hasn't got anything else to occupy himself with. But"—the manager's voice became confidential—"it might be something else. Suppose someone had a grudge against this camp and wanted to put us out of business? Suppose someone were after my job? Now what better way would there be to accomplish one of these goals than to spread a rumor like this?"

"I should think a story like that might help business," said Nelson shrewdly. "Wouldn't it attract a lot of curiosity seekers out here?"

"Yes, it would, and they'd come out in their cars and stand around close to them. But when it came to signing up for a cottage for a week or a month, they'd think about the children playing near the edge of the woods, and a leopard sneaking up and grabbing one of them and carrying him off—you see how ridiculous the whole thing sounds, but I'm showing you the fears people build up. They would pack up the children, carefully count noses to make sure no one was left, and drive off to spend their vacations somewhere else."

"Isn't it necessary to make reservations a long time ahead at a place like this?"

"Theoretically, yes, and of course the longer ahead, the better accommodations we can give. But we're a fairly new resort, and not usually overcrowded. We can still accommodate late-comers. And of course there is the matter of cancellations. We give full refund of the deposit if the cancellation is made forty-eight hours ahead."

"And you think if this leopard story gets out, you'll be getting a flood of cancellations?"

"That's exactly what I think. I was afraid of the story getting out, but with Mr. Jackson's loose tongue, it's out already."

"Then you have no objection to our talking with Mr. Jackson?"

"None at all. He's in number twenty-one. You'll probably find him there now, since it's close to suppertime. But if you don't find him, you can be sure he'll find you."

The boys picked up their luggage from the car, and started toward their cottage. Then they realized in what a far-off corner it was, and Nelson wondered if Mr. Armand had lodged them there deliberately.

"Look at all these empty cottages we're passing. He could have put us in one of them."

"Maybe not," Ted returned, trudging along, for the bags he was carrying were heavy. "They might be reserved, you know. But I don't think Mr. Armand plays either favors or grudges. He's got his own methodical way of doing things, and this is it."

"What do you think of a place like this, Ted?"

"A pretty expensive layout, I should say. Just think what the upkeep on it must come to. Then remember you're only full about three months a year, and maybe not that if you run into a long rainy spell. That means you've got to charge about four times as much as you would if the season were spread out over the year."

"It's a good way to gamble! Say, how do they arrange their meals around here?"

"Everybody cooks their own, I suppose, but they can buy anything they want down at the shop—even completely frozen dinners, if they want them. I saw the placard in the office. Do you want to get something while I look up Mr. Jackson?"

"What do you mean?" asked Nelson, crestfallen. "Don't you want me along?"

"Sure, I do. But I thought you might be getting anxious about eating or a swim."

"Not that anxious. The lake can wait, but maybe the leopard can't. It might vanish into thin air before I've even got a glimpse of it. You know, Ted, I don't expect it to happen, but wouldn't it be something if we did find a leopard? That's the sort of thing that doesn't happen every day."

"Did you think what you're going to hunt this leopard with?"

"Yes, and I decided you're right: the best thing to do would be to jump in the lake and swim for it."

"Well, I hope your leopard is accommodating enough to hang out near the water."

They had reached their cottage. Ted opened the door and they deposited their luggage inside, looked around a little, then came outside, and Ted locked up again.

"Isn't that lake something, Ted? How'd you like that for a skating rink?"

"Not very much. Look at the waves. It wouldn't freeze over very smoothly. And the water is too deep, in case you fall in."

"I wonder how deep it is?"

"If it's over six feet, which it surely is, then what's the difference? Let's not plan on falling in. I wonder if any of the vacationers swim across it? I suppose the camp tries to discourage it. It's always farther than it looks, and people don't realize their own limitations."

"Don't worry, I'm not planning on swimming across. I can't wait to get my tackle into that water, though. I think it's a state-stocked lake, so there ought to be something in it." He looked around at the trees, which came close up to the rear of the cottage, so that they were on the very edge of the woods. "This looks like a regular forest, Ted. There could be *something* in that woods, something big and terrible that we don't know about."

"Does that mean you're ready to believe in this leopard?"

"No, it just means that I feel a little differently about it than I did in Forestdale. Now let's go and find Mr. Jackson."

CHAPTER 3

THE TRACKS OF THE CAT

AT MR. JACKSON'S COTTAGE, the elderly man invited them to come inside. They found the cottage to be very much like their own, with the big difference that it looked settled and lived in. The furniture was attractive, the reading lights pleasant, and something very appetizing was sizzling on the stove. Their first impression of Mr. Jackson was that he must be about eighty years old, but later, observing how active the man seemed, Ted decided he was probably not quite as old as that.

Their host invited them to join him at supper, but though they were getting hungry, the boys declined, knowing that he hadn't been expecting visitors. Accepting their refusal with good nature, the old man continued with his preparations for the meal, and when it was ready, sat down to eat, motioning them into chairs.

"We came about the leopard," Ted remarked. He had previously given their names and the name of the paper, but wasn't sure Mr. Jackson had paid any attention. Now he realized that he had their names down pat.

"Yes, Ted, I know. I wouldn't have bothered calling the newspaper, but I found that that dunce of a manager didn't intend to do anything about it, so I had to prod him into motion. A leopard running around through the woods isn't something you can ignore for very long."

"How would a leopard get out there?" asked Nelson critically.

The old man shrugged. "Why do I have to answer that? If I showed you a dog in this room, for instance, you'd accept the fact that there was a dog. You wouldn't ask me where it came from and all about it, and if I couldn't answer refuse to believe there was a dog. Civilization is a funny thing. It has crowded out a good many forms of wild life, but pockets remain, and wild creatures turn up from time to time in the most unexpected places."

"But leopards don't live around here," Nelson observed. "If there is a leopard, it must have escaped from somewhere."

"Must it? All right, if you say so, but that's your observation—not mine."

Ted took over the questioning. "Just what proof do you have that there's a leopard around here?"

"The tracks, for one thing. You've heard about them?"

"Yes. Has anyone else seen these tracks besides you?"

"No. I told Mr. Armand, but he wasn't interested in going to look, so then I called the paper."

"He may have gone without telling you."

"I doubt that he could have found them without me to show him. In fact I didn't tell anyone else at all, because I felt they might stamp the ground all up before someone in authority could get there."

"You didn't see the leopard yourself?"

"Not I, but there are witnesses."

"Who are these witnesses?"

"There's a girl, Miss Holly Jergens."

"Is she the only one?" asked Ted, his eyes narrowing.

"There's her older brother, Gerald, too."

"Then he saw the leopard?"

"No, he didn't actually see it, but he knows that his sister wouldn't make up a story like this out of whole cloth. He'll back her up on it."

"How did you happen to find these tracks? Were you looking for them?"

"Yes. Miss Holly reported to her brother and me that she had seen some creature in the woods. She didn't use the word 'leopard,' but from the way she described it, we could tell that was what she meant. We rowed over there on Sunday, and that was when I found the tracks. I reported it to Mr. Armand, but when he wouldn't do anything about it, I called the newspaper this morning."

Mr. Jackson made it sound as though he had reported to the manager on Sunday, while Mr. Armand said it was Monday. Well, that was only a small detail, Ted decided.

"Now the way I understand it," he summarized, "no one has seen the leopard except Miss Holly. You later found these tracks, but I assume that you are no authority on tracks. If it hadn't been for the girl's story, you might never have thought of them as being leopard tracks. Isn't that right?"

"That didn't occur to me, young fellow, but I believe you're exactly right. Your paper's sent out a right smart man to look into this. I'm pleased to make your acquaintance."

"But surely this girl and her brother must have seen the tracks."

"Oh, no, I didn't show them either. They were with me, but I told them I wanted to get back to report it to the manager."

"Well, I guess there isn't much we can do, Mr. Jackson, until we've seen these tracks and talked with Miss Holly. I suppose you'd be willing to row across the lake with us and show us where the tracks are, and perhaps my friend could take pictures of them. How about early tomorrow morning?"

"What if it rains tonight? Don't you think we'd better get there before that happens?"

While it didn't exactly look like rain, it might come up. On the other hand, less than two hours of daylight remained, and hunting for leopard tracks at twilight wasn't the most sensible thing the boys had ever done.

"What do you say, Nel?"

"All right by me. Would we make better time driving the car around the lake?"

"No," Mr. Jackson informed them. "The road doesn't reach that far. We'll have a much shorter walk on the other side if we go by boat."

"All right, then, Mr. Jackson," Ted decided, "we'll get the camera and a bite to eat, and we'll be ready to leave in about twenty minutes. And thank you very much."

On the way back to their cottage, Nelson remarked with some disgust, "So that's all there is to it, just some hysterical girl's story, and we've come all this way on a fool's errand." He seemed disappointed, not over their trip, but that he wasn't going to find a leopard.

"Just because she's a girl doesn't mean she's wrong, Nel."

"Oh, I know that, but I don't think a girl would know the difference between a leopard and a bobcat."

"Even a bobcat would be unusual around here."

"I know, but I could believe in a bobcat. How would a leopard get here from Africa? I never heard of a leopard building a boat. And if it escaped, wouldn't the authorities have been notified by now? I wonder what Mr. Jackson's theory is?"

"He's looking for something bizarre, I'll bet, like a bobcat giving birth to a leopard through some sort of hereditary throwback. I know it's incredible, but incredible things are more interesting to him. Well, as he says, seeing the leopard is bettei evidence than explaining it."

"Let's stop for sandwiches, Ted, and we can eat them along the way. Do you think we ought to ask Mr. Armand if he wants to come along?"

"No, I don't. In the first place, the boat may not hold four. In the second place, he had his chance already. In the third place, I don't think he'd come."

"And in the fourth place, you want this story for yourself. Well, I don't blame you, but I can't get really thrilled about pictures. I might be able to sell pictures of a leopard, but I don't think I can sell pictures of tracks. Anyway, you don't really think we're going to find any tracks, do you, Ted?"

"Why not?"

"Because this whole thing is just some sort of gag. I don't know whether we're the victims, or someone else is, but that's the way it'll turn out. You'll find Mr. Jackson won't quite be able to find the place where he saw the tracks, or they'll be washed out or trampled over. And Miss Holly's story will be vague, and we won't be able to pin either of them down to anything."

Half an hour later they were ready to embark. Nelson put his camera carefully in the bottom of the boat, and took his place at the oars. Mr. Jackson took the seat beyond him, while Ted shoved the boat off into the water, then leaped for the prow. The water went over his shoetops, but he didn't mind. Skillfully, Nelson maneuvered them about, then set out for the long pull across the lake.

"If a leopard escaped from a zoo," Nelson remarked to Mr. Jackson, thinking he might be some sort of authority on the subject, "it wouldn't be very dangerous, would it? I mean, it would be used to people, and things like that. That ought to change the odds."

"Yes, I believe it would, Nelson—change the odds right against you. You see, an animal in the wild sets up certain habits and routines for itself, and it really doesn't vary them very much. A careful hunter can find out what those habits are, and he will be fairly safe as long as he works in conjunction with them. A zoo animal is quite different. When it finds itself on the loose, it is confused, not knowing whether to follow its tame habits, or its wild ones. And if the animal doesn't know what it is going to do next, how can a person know?"

"Well, just how dangerous is a leopard? Will it attack people? Can it climb very well? Can it swim?" Nelson asked.

"I don't think I'd care to trust any member of the cat family very far, and I imagine a hungry leopard would be particularly untrustworthy. I believe the leopard is one of the best climbers among the cats. I've read that it will carry heavy game up into a tree, out of reach of hyenas, and under certain conditions a leopard will lead an almost completely arboreal existence. As for swimming, most cats seem to be able to swim well enough if they make up their minds to it."

"Wow!" said Nelson involuntarily, his plans for escape from a possible leopard having been dealt a severe blow. "What time of day does a leopard like to hunt? Does it prefer the light or the dark?"

"I don't think there is any hard-and-fast rule about it. A leopard, of course, possesses the cat's ability to see very well in a dim light. But in the long run it has to hunt at whatever time the game it is seeking is out—daytime for squirrels, night time for rats, and so on."

"I wonder what time of day I'd feel safer if I were being hunted?" Ted speculated. "In the daylight you could be seen more easily, but you could also watch out more carefully for something that was attacking."

"You'd be safer in the light, Ted, because you depend so much on your eyes. In the night you would be relatively helpless against a strong animal that could hear and smell much better than you. Nature has to balance all those things out, when she gives her creatures their particular set of attributes."

"What about twilight?" asked Nelson. "I've heard that some animals like to hunt then, while the other animals are visiting the water holes."

"That may be true of wild animals. A zoo animal would be more erratic, and particularly if it were very hungry, would be dangerous all the time."

Nelson grunted, but whether this was from the exertion of rowing or a comment was not clear. It was taking quite a while to get across the lake, and it was apparent now that the light would be dim by the time they got beneath the trees. Ted wondered if Mr. Jackson would be able to find the tracks after all. It had not seemed necessary to bring a flashlight or a lantern as long as Mr. Jackson knew exactly where to find the tracks.

When they landed on the far shore and drew the boat up to a safe position, Mr. Jackson pointed out the path they were to take, and seemed to know what he was doing. Nelson cast some furtive glances about, particularly observing the low overhanging branches above the path. He didn't really believe there was a leopard, but if there was, he was no more apprehensive about it than the others. His eagerness to know all the details about the possible danger they faced stemmed from another source. If danger developed, he expected to take the lead in meeting it. Certainly he could rely on no help at all from Mr. Jackson, and while Ted had his share of daring and would back Nelson up, still he tended to be a somewhat more careful person than Nelson.

"Is it much farther?" Ted inquired, for the shadows were deepening all about them.

"No, not much—I think." For the first time their guide seemed confused. "It should be right about here somewhere."

"Hum," Nelson was heard to murmur.

Mr. Jackson continued to lead the way, but in a somewhat uncertain fashion. Quite abruptly he turned down another path, and the boys followed. Suddenly he stopped and indicated a slight dip in the path not far beyond.

The boys hurried past him and stared down into the mud with straining eyes. There were certainly tracks of some sort, the prints of some huge cat. Nelson immediately prepared to take some pictures.

CHAPTER 4

DOUBLES FOR TENNIS

Having returned to their cottage, Nelson set about getting his photographic equipment in order, while Ted opened their suitcases and began to unpack.

"What do you want me to do with these films, Ted?"

"The sooner you can get them processed, the better."

"I thought I noticed a place in the village that advertised overnight service. But then what? You going to send them back to Mr. Dobson?"

"No. What good would that do? He wouldn't be able to tell what those tracks are any better than we can. But I'd like to get an expert opinion on this business. I think there's a zoo in Weatherby—that's about the only town around here large enough to support one."

"Weatherby's a good fifteen or eighteen miles away, Ted. I know that's not far by car, but it's pretty far for a leopard to make its way through the woods without being spotted, particularly if it had to pass through some small communities on the way."

Ted considered. "I know it's difficult, but any other zoo would be farther away, and that would make it even more difficult. I don't really think a leopard escaped from Weatherby, or from anywhere, for that matter. But there's something out in the woods, and we've got pictures of the tracks to prove it. For the time being I'm going to assume that it's a lynx, or something like that—unusual around here and exceptionally big, but not impossible. The zoo at Weatherby ought to have a curator or keeper of some sort, and he may be able to back up my theory."

"Your theory doesn't include Miss Holly Jergens," Nelson pointed out.

"I know. I'll try to talk with her tomorrow morning. Then we'll be ready to run up to Weatherby."

After Nelson had gone, Ted continued with the unpacking, since it wouldn't take long, and they would need some things for the night. Their cottage was equipped with a small refrigerator and a compact stove, and he decided he might as well do the week's shopping right away, since they would have to cook breakfast at least. Returning from the store, he put his purchases away. Nelson still had not returned, so he strolled outside and down toward the beach. He walked along the shore for a while, then returned to the cottage. He made himself a little lunch, then decided he might as well go to bed but he was still awake when Nelson came in.

"Lucky to get here," the amateur photographer remarked. "Did you know the gates are locked at ten o'clock? I had to press the night button to get somebody to let me in, and then he looked me over like I was smuggling weapons into a prison."

"When will the pictures be ready?"

"Eleven o'clock in the morning. Did you get any milk? I could do with a glass."

He not only found the milk, but crackers and peanut butter besides.

"Ted, what do you think of Mr. Jackson?"

"I'll know better after I've talked to Miss Holly."

"You mean he might have faked the footprints, and you want to find out if he could have helped fake her story, too?"

"Is that what I mean? It does sound a little like it," Ted returned sleepily.

"You know, I thought it was funny the way he answered all my questions about leopards. Is he really an authority on the subject, or what?"

"I imagine that as soon as this leopard scare came up, he read everything he could on the subject. I suppose that makes him an authority—anyway, a two-day authority."

"Nearly a full moon tonight. Do leopards like to hunt in the moonlight?" Nelson wondered.

"I don't know. Ask Mr. Jackson," and Ted turned over noisily to let his friend know he was tired and wanted to sleep.

They both slept well, having put in a long and strenuous day. But Nelson was awakened during the night by something he could never afterward quite describe. Aroused suddenly, he sat up in bed and listened carefully. But the sound, whatever it was, was not repeated. Nelson eased himself down into bed again, and finally fell asleep.

He mentioned it to Ted in the morning, but Ted either had not heard it or had immediately fallen asleep again and could not remember.

"What did it sound like?" he questioned.

"I don't exactly know—but sort of—like a leopard's cry!"

"How does a leopard sound?" Ted demanded.

"I don't know. I never heard one."

"Then how do you know it was a leopard?"

This stumped Nelson, but only momentarily. "Well, it was *like* a cry a leopard ought to make when it's hunting. I know I never heard a leopard before, but I never heard anything like this, either."

"I thought the leopard was supposed to be on the other side of the lake. How do you think it got over here? If it walked around the south end of the lake, it would have a long, long hike. And if it walked around the north end, it would have to cross the dam."

"Don't you think we could hear it from across the lake, if the wind was right?"

"I think you were dreaming," Ted maintained.

And while Nelson was willing to admit that he may have had leopards on his mind and possibly in his dreams, he still insisted he had heard *something*—something out there in the forest night.

"And it was something that didn't belong there, too!"

Soon after breakfast there came a knock on their door. Answering, they found a young man there, dressed in white clothes and carrying a tennis racket.

"I'm Gerald Jergens, and you must be Ted Wilford and Nelson Morgan. Mr. Jackson told us about you. Any chance I could interest you in doubles tennis? My sister Holly will be along in a minute. Or are you busy with something else?"

"No, we're not doing anything else," Ted informed him.

"Until eleven o'clock," Nelson corrected.

"Well, then, what would you say to a few sets?"

"I'll watch," Nelson decided. "At tennis I'm a regular rock-head."

"Oh, but we need you if we're going to play doubles. Here comes Holly now."

She came up to the door, and her brother made the introductions. She seemed a little younger than they were, just as her brother seemed a little older, so they fitted nicely between.

"You're the girl who saw the leopard, aren't you?" asked Nelson, as, rackets in hand, the four of them started down toward the courts.

"I suppose Mr. Jackson told you everything," Gerald interposed. "Holly and I decided not to say anything about it, but you can't stop a man like Mr. Jackson from talking. Several other persons have told us they heard about it, too."

"But it doesn't seem to have caused much of a panic around here," Ted noted.

"Oh, no, not yet. It is just an idle rumor so far. But if other people report seeing it, then you might have a kind of panic or exodus."

A silence fell, as they waited for Holly to answer Nelson's earlier question. She took her time, and tried to reply carefully.

"I didn't tell anybody I saw a leopard, if that is what it was. All I said was that I had seen a large animal with spots."

"If it wasn't a leopard, then what was it—a Dalmatian?" Nelson noted a scowl from Ted, and subsided.

"How did you happen to see it?" Ted asked the girl.

"Well, I rowed across the lake, just for exercise. Then I thought I might as well get out and look around a little. I'm particularly interested in wild flowers, and decided I'd explore awhile. I thought it would be perfectly safe, since no one had mentioned any kind of danger around here. I must have wandered quite a way into the woods, when I happened to look up, and there was this—this animal, standing directly on the path in front of me, and grinning. It looked at me for a moment, then turned around and ran away."

"You didn't see where it went?"

"No. Oh, I admit I didn't try very hard. For a moment I was too startled to do anything, and in fact I didn't really get scared until I got home and told Gerald and Mr. Jackson. They thought it sounded like a leopard."

"*Mr. Jackson* thought so," Gerald corrected. "I don't have any opinion about it."

"Did it leap into the trees, or just run down the path?" Nelson questioned.

"I think it just ran down the path until it was out of sight. I'm not sure, though."

"Is it possible that it was simply a large lynx?" asked Ted.

"A lynx—that's the animal very much like a bobcat, isn't it? I understand the name comes from its short, bobbed tail. But this animal had a very long tail. I'm pretty sure about that."

"Then you went back the next day to look for the animal again and found tracks?"

"Mr. Jackson found the tracks. Gerald and I didn't see them. We had separated a little. That was Mr. Jackson's idea, but Gerald wasn't very eager to leave me alone so he was close to me. Then Mr. Jackson called out that he had found the tracks. We wanted to see them, too, but he seemed in a hurry to get back and report the matter to Mr. Armand, and see if he wouldn't do something about it. You went to see the tracks yourselves, didn't you?"

"Yes, and we took pictures of them. We're waiting for them to be printed right now. Then we plan to look up the director of the Weatherby zoo and see if he can identify them."

"You're a newspaper reporter, aren't you, Ted? Mr. Jackson mentioned that you were."

"Well, I work for a country newspaper," Ted admitted.

"That must be thrilling work."

"It has its moments," he agreed.

"We're in luck," Gerald cried. "There's an empty court, so we won't have to wait. Come on, you take Holly, Ted, and I'll take the rockhead."

Gerald was easily the best player of the four. Whether he was holding back Ted could not tell, and would have liked to see him play sometime against a worthy opponent. Ted and Holly were about equal in ability, but both surpassed the hapless Nelson. He had played very little tennis before, and his inexperience was obvious.

However, the two teams were well matched, and Ted and Holly finally won two of the three sets played.

"We'll have to try it again soon," Gerald remarked to the others, and they all agreed that they would.

"And now to drink about a gallon of water," said Nelson to Ted as they headed back toward their cottage, "and then off for the pictures. I can see you're getting perked up about this leopard yarn now."

"Why now especially?"

"Because Holly didn't turn out to be the hysterical female you thought she was going to be. I admit her story sounded pretty good to me, too. She seemed to be trying to be very careful to tell us just what she saw. And she wouldn't even claim it was a leopard. It seemed to be Mr. Jackson who was trying to talk her into that."

"Well, what do you think of the whole thing now?"

"Oh, I think she's made a mistake of some sort. I don't think she's lying, or imagining things, or deliberately exaggerating. But she could easily be wrong. It's hard to judge exactly how large an animal is unless you are right up near it, and on a forest path the sunlight is uneven, and might easily suggest spots."

"What about the tail?"

"Well, she did seem pretty sure about that tail, didn't she? But what was wrong with my idea about a Dalmatian dog? I saw that dirty look you gave me."

"Don't you think she'd know a dog by now if she saw one? Anyway, she emphasized afterward how much it looked like a cat. And while she didn't come right out and say it was a leopard, you could tell she hadn't seen anything that would contradict the idea of a leopard. I'll tell you how I think it is. She's a sensible girl, and she knows how unlikely it is for a leopard to be roaming through the woods here, but at the same time her image of the animal suggests a leopard to her. She's caught right in the middle between her common sense and what she thinks she saw."

"Maybe the pictures will settle the thing for us, Ted."

"I hope so, but I kind of doubt it. I have an idea that all cat tracks look pretty much alike. The zoo keeper may be able to tell us whether it's a member of the cat family or not, and that may be as far as he's willing to go. . . . Well, me for a quick shower and a change of clothes, and we'll get on our way."

"Right!" Nelson agreed readily. "We'll never know more than we do now, unless we get a move on."

CHAPTER 5

FOUR OF A KIND

The pictures turned out to be clear and sharp, and Nelson found only one fault with them.

"You can't tell how large the footprints are on the pictures, Ted. If we'd only thought, we could have put one of our own footprints alongside. Why didn't you think of it? You're supposed to be the brainboy around here."

"That sounds more like footwork than headwork," said Ted with a grin.

"Think we ought to go back and do it again?"

"No, that would tie us up for another day. I'm not sure we could even find them without Mr. Jackson, and it looks like we may have a sprinkle soon anyway. But I did use my head about one thing. I measured one of the prints, remember?"

"Well, maybe that will do it."

Arriving at the zoo in Weatherby, they were shown to the office of the director, Dr. Larken, who had agreed over the telephone to talk with them. He studied the pictures, and listened carefully to their story of Holly's seeing a strange animal in the wood.

"You've given me a pretty difficult assignment," he said at last. "These pictures were taken by flashlight, were they not?" He indicated the darkening of the picture toward its borders.

"Yes," Nelson informed him. "There was a little daylight left, but not enough for the pictures, so I had to use the flash. Does that make any difference?"

"Not much. The slanting sun might have cast a shadow which would give me a better indication of their depth, but it wouldn't do much good unless I knew the character of the soil. I'll have to tell you frankly that most of what I learned about tracking came to me as a farm boy. Since then most of my knowledge has come from books, but I think the boy learned more than the man."

"Can you tell what kind of animal it is?" asked Nelson.

"Now there you're certainly putting me on a spot, Morgan. The tracks themselves are not too sharp, which is to be expected in a soft surface. But the pads do strongly indicate the cat family, rather than the dog family, for example. You've given me the dimensions of one of the tracks, but of course this isn't too accurate. When you've made tracks in the snow, you've observed that the prints you leave are actually larger than your feet, while on the other hand, in a soft, flowing surface the mud will tend to move in around the edges. The gait of the animal might be helpful, but that's not apparent from your pictures. Another point is that the size of the tracks does not always indicate the size of the creature. You've seen some dogs with unusually large and floppy feet. The age of the animal is another factor, since in a young animal the feet may be larger in proportion to body build than in an older animal.

"But taking all these things into consideration, I would still have to say that these tracks were made by some member of the cat family larger than anything which is native to this region. But I must add a word of caution. It might have been an unusually large member of its species. Something like this occasionally happens with human beings, and it is even more prevalent among animals. There are some animals which seem to have no built-in limitation on their size, but continue to grow throughout their lifetimes. So while this could be an exceptionally large lynx, I still consider it highly improbable."

"Well, if it isn't a native animal, what sort might it be?" Nelson questioned.

The doctor smiled and shook his head. "Don't expect too much of me, Morgan. I'm certainly not an expert on the tracks of all members of the cat family throughout the world—even if your pictures were clear enough, which they are not. Creatures of the same species vary a great deal from region to region. So now we must consider the other evidence available. Your witness mentioned spots and a long tail. That means it could be a leopard, although I can't say definitely. Of course I can't understand how a leopard could be roaming through your woods, but I am equally at a loss to understand how any other creature which could have made these tracks could be there either. May I ask how reliable your witness is?"

Ted and Nelson exchanged quick glances. "I think she's as reliable as most witnesses," said Ted slowly.

"Well, if that is true, Wilford, it isn't a hoax. I was thinking that these might not be real tracks. Is this all the evidence you have?"

"I thought maybe I heard it howling last night," said Nelson, a little lamely.

"You did?" asked Dr. Larken with interest. "How did it sound?"

Nelson looked a trifle embarrassed, but given sufficient encouragement he tried to imitate the sound he had heard. "You must have heard it, too, Ted," he urged his friend. "You were about half awake."

But Ted denied that he had ever heard anything like that, either in this world or out of it, and the doctor smiled. "What ever you heard, Morgan, I have my doubts that it was a leopard. The leopard is a notoriously quiet hunter, except when it is actually on the attack.

"I think you can be pretty sure of one thing," he went on. "If there really is some such animal roaming through your woods, it will soon be heard from again. If so, and you've got a little more reliable testimony than you've got now, I wish you'd let me know. I can't afford to leave my work and look into the matter on the basis of what you've told me so far, but a little more evidence would strongly tempt me. Now would you care to look through our cat collection as long as you're here?"

The boys agreed that they certainly would, and he accompanied them down to the cages. The zoo had a very fine leopard, and they stood in front of the cage and admired it for some minutes.

"Does it ever howl?" Nelson questioned the director.

"Not often. You might try that call of yours and see if you can get any response."

Nelson looked around. There were no other visitors in the building just then, and he felt encouraged to try. He repeated the call he claimed he had heard, but the leopard paid no attention to him at all, although a bird somewhere began to squawk.

"I take it you're not missing a leopard?" Ted inquired.

"No. If we were, you may be certain I would have notified the authorities at once."

"Are there any other zoos around here a leopard might have escaped from?"

"There's one in Alabaster, but of course that's about thirty miles from Vanishing Lake. And if you were to inquire there, I have no doubt you'd get the same response that you got here—there's no leopard missing. It really isn't possible to keep such a thing secret for very long, and I don't think any public institution would try it, though a small, private show might."

"Might not the director of a zoo feel the escape of an animal would reflect on him, so he'd be anxious to recover the animal without publicity?"

"Possibly, but I don't think the director of any public zoo would attempt to operate on such a basis. As a matter of fact, if an animal escaped, the blame would probably rest with one of the keepers rather than the director. But even if the director was at fault, how could he hope to keep it secret? Remember that he has a staff working under him, and someone would almost certainly let the news out, some employee who felt he was performing a public service by alerting the public. And then there is always a chance—a high probability in the case of a larger animal—of the creature being sighted publicly. Quite possibly no one could blame the director for the escape, but he certainly could be blamed for concealing the news, and dismissal would be almost certain. No, I simply do not believe any director would do such a thing."

"And anyway the likelihood of a leopard making its way fifteen or thirty miles through partly built-up country would almost rule the whole thing out."

"Well, now, just a moment, Wilford. I'm not anxious to build up this leopard idea of yours, but I think your last argument was rather weak. You mention the difficulty of a wild animal traveling so far without discovery. Have you ever thought of the difficulty of a wild animal's finding its way *back* through difficult countryside? Let's suppose a leopard escaped and tried to travel through the woods, either out of curiosity or through the necessity of seeking out food. It can be supposed that the animal would encounter difficulties here, a scare or a narrow escape there. While its normal instinct would be to try to return to its original place, which must represent some feeling of security to it, still the difficulties and frights encountered would have the effect of urging it to go on, rather than return. Provided that the problems are not *too* great, the animal might push on a great distance from its point of origin. The obstacles, rather than hindering it, actually force it on."

This was a novel point of view, but with a certain validity, Ted decided as he thought it over carefully.

Dr. Larken allowed them to peek in at a mother lion and her four playful cubs. They were being kept screened off from the public because, as he explained, the mother was still nervous.

They stopped to watch one of the zoo's tigers, but the animal seemed sleepy and not much interested in them. It was quite a warm day.

"I wonder what it's dreaming about—the jungle?" Nelson pondered.

"Hardly. It's never even seen the jungle, for it was raised in captivity. Life in a cage does allow plenty of time to think, though what the animals think about I couldn't guess."

But Nelson was not convinced that an animal might not long for a jungle it had never seen, some instinct telling it of another way of life for which it was better suited. However, there was no time to argue the matter, for it was past Dr. Larken's lunchtime, and the boys were growing hungry, too. They decided to call it a day.

"Come back and visit us again soon," the doctor invited them. "The animals enjoy looking at people," and on this note the group broke up.

"Are you getting too hungry, or do you want to wait till we get to camp?" Nelson asked as they rode toward the lake.

"Why not wait? We're almost there."

"But then we'll have to cook it and—" He stopped and nodded toward a rising column of smoke. "If somebody's planning a cook out, he must have some awfully big wieners."

CHAPTER 6

WAVING GRASS

As they drove into the camp parking lot, the boys were able to spot the fire burning just beyond the edge of the row of cottages. The fire engine from the village was already on the scene, having driven across the lawns and footpaths to the site, but Nelson did not dare to follow this example. The boys took off at a sprint to reach the crowd of spectators.

The flames, though still spectacular, seemed to have been brought under control on the sides toward the woods and cottages, and would soon disappear harmlessly as they reached the edge of the lake.

"A good thing it was spotted in time," Mr. Armand remarked to the fire chief.

"And we were lucky with the wind, too," the chief pointed out. "Had it been blowing toward the cottages or toward the woods, there might not have been much we could do. But fortunately it was blowing straight out toward the lake, so the fire didn't have much place to go."

"What's in that little shack?" asked Ted of the manager, indicating a small building which stood between the fire and the lake, and would soon be sacrificed to the flames.

"Just a shed for tools, and for camp equipment when we don't want to carry it all the way to the other end of the camp. We just looked inside. There's nothing in there worth trying to save."

The small village fire department had been able to handle the job, but had the fire grown, it might have taken too long to summon help from the surrounding villages, and the camp might have faced disaster. Mr. Armand expressed his thanks to all the firemen, through their chief, and offered them refreshments.

"We have to get back as soon as we can," the chief explained, "but I guess we'll have time for coffee. This fire will take us another fifteen minutes yet. Meanwhile, I can make a few inquiries about the cause of the fire."

Without appearing intrusive, Ted was able to maneuver fairly close to the chief as he talked with the persons who had first spotted the flames. But no useful information was forthcoming. The witnesses had no idea how the fire had started or how long it may have smoldered before they observed it. The chief shrugged.

"That's the way most of these things turn out. We're not trying to blame anyone, but simply trying to prevent the same thing from happening again. And of course there's a report to fill out for insurance and statistical purposes."

They were interrupted just then by a woman who rushed up to the manager exclaiming:

"I can't find my Jimmy anywhere. Have you seen him? I've called and called, but there wasn't any answer. And I checked with the lifeguard, but he hasn't been seen on the beach, and I don't think he'd go there anyway because he doesn't care much for the water."

Mr. Armand looked as though a lost child was the least of his worries at that moment, but he was forced to be polite.

"I'm sure he'll show up soon, and I'll put my staff to work looking for him."

Suddenly Ted lowered his head and dashed through the smoke toward the tool shed. He pushed open the door. As the manager had said, there seemed to be nothing of value in there, but the door did not open all the way. There was some obstacle behind it. Ted looked behind the door, and there sat a little boy, obstinately quiet, a pout on his face, oblivious to the approaching danger. Ted grabbed up the boy, and protecting him from the smoke as much as possible, ran back to the group of spectators and safety.

The mother grasped the boy in her arms, torn between tears and laughter.

"Jimmy!" she exclaimed. When she was able to speak more calmly, she explained to the others, "I scolded him a little while ago, and I suppose he went off to hide and pout." She turned to Ted. "I can't tell you how grateful I am. I don't know how you thought of that."

"It wasn't hard. I'm sure someone else would soon have thought of it."

"Sure, we all would," Nelson agreed, "but maybe about ten minutes too late."

"I have to get to my husband now—he's searching in the other direction—and I'm sure he'll want to have a talk with you later."

As she left them, the manager remarked bitterly, "People should be able to keep track of their own children. If anything had happened to that child, we might as well have closed down the camp for the rest of the season."

This seemed very unfeeling, but as Mr. Armand turned away to talk with the fire chief, Nelson remarked:

"I suppose he's got money on his mind. Maybe he only gets a small salary, but earns a bonus if there are so many guests during the season, or the camp makes a certain profit."

"Oh, I think he was really upset about the boy," Ted returned in a low voice, "but he's trying to blame somebody else."

With the fire finally extinguished, the firemen drove off, while the campers gave them a cheer of appreciation. Although the incident might easily have ended in tragedy, everything was all right now, and people were trying to forget the terrible possibilities.

Nelson had located Gerald and Holly.

"You were wonderful, Ted," Holly exclaimed. "I wonder why you thought about the boy being in the shed before anybody else did?"

Ted felt his face growing uncomfortably red. "I don't believe I thought about anything—I just acted without thinking. But the truth is, I used to be a hideaway boy like that myself."

"You were?" said Nelson in disbelief. "And here I thought you always were a brain."

"Oh, I've done plenty of stupid things, and sometimes I'm glad, because then I can understand the stupid things that other people do."

Mr. Armand came over to join the group.

"Find out anything about your leopard?" he asked, showing that he had been well aware of the nature of their excursion that morning. Evidently Mr. Jackson, who knew what the boys intended to do with the pictures, had told him.

"Well, we got a lot of information," said Nelson cheerfully.

"But no leopard?"

"No, not for sure."

"But I think there's been enough evidence so that we ought to look into it further," Ted stated.

"What evidence?" the manager demanded. "Some footprints that evidently you were unable to identify, and—" He stopped when he noticed Holly in the group, deciding it would be more tactful not to mention the possibility that she was either lying or seriously mistaken.

"Well, it's certain that *some* large animal made those tracks," Ted pointed out.

"Why not a large dog? That wouldn't be anything particularly remarkable."

"The zoo keeper at Weatherby didn't seem to think it was a dog."

"But he wasn't sure?"

"No. But as long as there is this uncertainty about it, wouldn't it be better to try to clear the whole thing up?"

"I can't stop you young men from doing anything you please, but just how does this concern me?"

"Couldn't we organize a little expedition," Ted suggested, "sort of beat our way through the woods and see if we can stir up anything? I suppose I got that idea from a movie, but it seems to be the way they do it. The natives advance in a long line, beating on pans and making a lot of noise—"

Mr. Armand's expression was a mixture of amusement and disdain. "And just how many beaters do the producers employ when they're filming a scene of this sort? Whatever the number, I assure you I don't have a budget sufficient for financing a Grade A motion picture."

"How many could you spare?" asked Nelson.

"About six at the most."

"Well, that wouldn't be so bad. Maybe a few of the men campers would come along with us—"

"And maybe they wouldn't," Mr. Armand snapped. "If I thought there was really any danger, I couldn't allow it, and if there isn't, it would seem too stupid to ask them. Anyway, I haven't said I'd go." He motioned with his arm toward the destruction caused by the fire, mostly underbrush and sapplings, but leaving a rather unsightly mess. "Don't you think we've got enough to do around here? Now if you had any new evidence to offer, something to suggest that there really might be a leopard or some similar animal out there—"

Nelson looked at Ted, who gave a slight shrug to indicate it was up to Nelson to decide. Taking this for a sign of encouragement, Nelson told about the cry he had heard during the night. To the boys' surprise, Holly showed unusual excitement.

"Oh, did you hear it, too? Something like that awakened me during the night, but I thought it was a child screaming."

"So that's your new evidence, a child with a nightmare," said Mr. Armand with as much sarcasm as he dared use toward paying guests.

They seemed to be at an impasse. Ted and Nelson were wondering what they could do next. Of course there was nothing to stop them from exploring on their own, but a larger party would have meant a much better chance for success. Besides, they were handicapped by unfamiliarity with the woods. So the five people stood in a silent group for a moment, waiting for a final decision to be made. At this moment, just as Mr. Armand seemed about to take his leave, they were joined by another man, one of the guests the boys had noticed before.

"Mr. Armand," he said abruptly, without waiting for introductions, "I thought I heard you mention the word 'leopard.' I know there've been stories going around about a leopard in the woods, but I didn't put much stock in them till this morning. I rowed across the lake with my son and a friend of his. We took off for a little hike through the woods"—he gestured in the approximate direction where the tracks had been found—"and we came to a kind of grass meadow up on a plateau. It's almost treeless there."

The manager nodded. "I know where you mean."

"The two boys are junior explorers, and they've been sort of trained to notice things. They called my attention to the way the top of the grass was blowing, and began to ask me various questions about the wind. But of course it was obvious to me that it wasn't the wind doing it at all. There was some large animal creeping along through the grass!"

The three young men caught their breaths in a gasp of surprise, but Holly looked triumphant. She could hardly have escaped noticing that her story had lain under a cloud of doubt, and she was glad to find some confirmation.

Mr. Armand, on the other hand, looked more exasperated than ever. "But I don't suppose either you or the boys actually saw any animal at all, let alone a leopard."

"Well, no. I just turned around and eased them off that plateau without letting on there was anything wrong. They still think it was the wind. I didn't feel I had any right to hang around and try to verify my deduction, when I had two youngsters under my care." He spoke a little vindictively, as though someone had accused him of cowardice.

The camp manager's attitude immediately became soothing. "I'm sure you did exactly right, Mr. Krause. If there was any danger, your responsibility was toward the boys. But this whole thing is becoming very annoying—an elusive leopard, or some animal, whom no one quite sees, or," glancing at Holly, "at least not very clearly."

His tone sounded indecisive once more, in contrast to the flat turndown he had given the boys' proposition previously, and they felt it might be a good time to push their idea once more.

"Don't you think we ought to see what we can find out about it?" Ted urged him.

"Well—as long as the guests are beginning to become alarmed, I suppose I really don't have any choice. I wish I knew what Mr. Gordon would have to say about it, though." Ted gathered that Mr. Gordon was the owner of the resort. "He'll be here tomorrow. Unfortunately, he's on the road right now, so I have no way of reaching him."

"Then wouldn't it be better if you could clear up the whole thing before he gets here?" Nelson argued.

"I suppose it would—if I thought this plan of yours would clear it up. Unfortunately, I don't see how it can. If we don't find a leopard—and of course we won't—that still won't prove conclusively that there *isn't* a leopard. However, I suppose I'd better do it. I can at least let Mr. Gordon know that I *tried* to do something about it."

"Shall some of us go along?" asked Mr. Krause.

"No, thank you, Mr. Krause. I'm sure Mr. Gordon would never approve of that."

"What about us?" Nelson called, as Mr. Armand turned and started away.

"Well," he called back over his shoulder, "I don't suppose I can keep members of the press away, or they'd never give me any peace afterward. Be at the parking lot in half an hour." He continued on, apparently concerned over the deep tracks the fire engine had made across some of the carefully kept lawns.

"Well, you boys have all the luck," said Gerald enviously. "I suppose he couldn't stop us from rowing across the lake ourselves, but I guess I won't. Mr. Armand's running things, so we ought to give him a chance to run them the way he wants to. Or does that sound like I'm trying to get out of it?"

But it was obvious from his tone that he wasn't trying to get out of anything, and his friends hastened to reassure him of that fact.

"But this may not be the end of it," Ted felt obliged to say. "If there is a leopard, and if we do find it, I don't think we'll be able to make any plans for capturing it immediately. Somehow I don't think this is going to be the last of the leopard, today."

Until now, Holly's eyes had glowed with the excitement of the hunt, but all at once her expression sobered as she realized that there might be some danger after all.

"Oh, Ted, you must be careful, because"—they had started, two by two, back toward the cabins, and her voice sank to a whisper that only Ted heard—"I really did see an animal that looked like a leopard, Ted."

"I'm sure you did, Holly. That's what gave me an incentive to keep after the story."

"But Ted, if I should be wrong, and this whole thing turns out to be a false lead, what is your editor going to say?"

Ted smiled. "Don't worry about that. Mr. Dobson is a very understanding man."

Their short walk had taken them to the Jergens' cottage, and the foursome was obliged to break up.

"Doubles tennis, the first chance you get," Gerald called in parting, and his friends promised to remember.

The boys, having eaten quickly, couldn't decide what to take along on the leopard hunt. They had no weapons of any kind, and would have had no skill at using them, even if they had.

"But a baseball bat might not be a bad thing," Nelson mused. "I could stop and buy one at the store, if you wanted one."

But Ted had little confidence they could beat off a determined leopard with a baseball bat, and anyway they agreed they would feel rather silly setting out on a leopard hunt with such a weapon.

"If we need it, we can probably pick up a club in the woods that will be just as good," Ted decided. "What about noise? Ought we to beat on pans or something like that to rouse the leopard, or have I been seeing too many movies?"

They talked it over, and decided that while noise might be a good idea, they would feel even sillier beating on pans than they would carrying a baseball bat. Somehow, though he hadn't said so, they suspected Mr. Armand of having a condescending attitude toward their youth and inexperience, and were anxious to appear grown up and confident in his eyes. And they could still manage to make plenty of noise with calls and shouts and perhaps beating the underbrush with a long stick.

Finally they decided not to take anything along on the hunt. Nelson even decided—with noticeable reluctance—against taking his camera.

"I don't think there's much chance of getting a good picture, and it'll just be something to hinder me."

"You could leave it locked up in the car," Ted suggested.

"I could leave it locked up better here. Anyway, the lock on my trunk compartment is broken."

"You could lock it in the car itself."

"Somebody can always get in there by breaking a window, if he wants to badly enough."

"If there is anybody out there to steal it."

"Oh, there probably is. Everybody isn't scared to pieces about this leopard."

They left the cottage, and started the rather long walk toward the parking lot at the other end of the camp. Ted nodded back toward the scene of the fire.

"What do you think about that, Nel?"

"Think about it? Somebody got careless with a cigarette, I suppose. That's usually the way of it—or at least that's what usually gets the blame."

"I'm wondering, though—first this leopard business, and now the fire. Does that suggest a pattern to you?"

"What sort of pattern, Ted?" asked Nelson with interest.

"As though there were something about this camp that is attracting bad luck toward it."

"Gosh, do you really think so?"

"I don't know yet. Could be. Well, let's skip it till we see how this leopard business comes out."

CHAPTER 7

THE LEOPARD HUNT

Mr. Armand had rounded up five employees, besides himself, who were waiting as the boys reached the parking lot.

"We'll go across in my car," Mr. Armand directed. "You young men can pile in with us, or go in your own car, whichever you prefer."

"We'll take our car," Nelson informed him.

"Very well. I should tell you that none of us are armed. I insisted upon this point, because I believe the danger of one of us getting shot accidentally, in case there is some sort of excitement, would be far greater than the danger from a leopard. If there is a leopard. I have a few more instructions, but they can wait till we get across the lake."

Without further comment, the men climbed into the car and followed by Nelson and Ted took off along the road leading around the end of the lake. At the extremity of the lake they crossed over a small plank bridge which spanned a creek feeding into the lake.

"Is this all that's feeding this big lake?" asked Ted incredulously.

"There may be others, but this could do it alone. It doesn't matter how much water you put in, as long as you don't have more coming out. Looks like a good spot to fish, though."

Having crossed the bridge, they could regard themselves as being on the other side of the lake. The road did not extend very far beyond, and they presently caught up with the leading car, from which the men had already dismounted.

"Now here's how we'll do it," Mr. Armand explained crisply when they reached the take-off point. "We'll start from here, and head directly into the woods. We'll keep in a long row as," he glanced out of the side of his eyes at Ted, "this young man saw them do in the movies. He also suggested that we make a lot of noise. I'm not so sure about that. If we were on a real hunt, the idea would be to keep as quiet as possible to avoid startling the game, but this is rather different, and he may be right about it. However, I've brought each of us a whistle, and you can blow on them as much as you please." He distributed a whistle to each one.

"Now the real purpose of these whistles is to help us keep together. Let's count off. I'm one." The men took up the count, and Nelson came out seven, with Ted eight. "From time to time, since we may get out of sight of each other, it might be wise to take a roll call to make sure everyone is all right. I'll blow once, number two will blow twice, and so on. And if it should be desirable to assemble, or any danger should appear, we'll blow three times."

"That'll be the same as the third man's other signal," Nelson pointed out.

"You're right about that. Then let's make that three *long* blasts for the danger signal. Any questions?"

"If a leopard comes leaping at me," Nelson muttered to Ted, "my three blasts aren't going to be very long."

But Ted found himself dissatisfied with the entire arrangement. While it was true that they were on the same side of the lake on which the tracks had been found, they were up at one end, while the tracks had appeared down near the other end. He pointed out this fact to Mr. Armand, to find the manager impatient as usual.

"I'm only going through with this to satisfy you boys," he exclaimed. "I'm sure that if there is a leopard, it must cover a wide range in its search for food, of which there would certainly be a scarcity, so that it's just as likely to be at one place as another."

"But not while we're here," Nelson observed.

"I can't help that," said Mr. Armand sharply. "I've only got so many men to work with, and this is the best I can do. We'll go ahead with my plan. We'll start into the woods here, then as we near the end we'll take a big horseshoe turn and come back again. That will cover the woods just as thoroughly as our manpower—and I may add, our time—will permit, and at the end we'll be very close to the place where Mr. Jackson said he found the tracks. Besides, it may not be necessary to actually see the leopard. We may find more tracks, or some place where it's nested or holed up, or a partially eaten kill, or other forms of evidence. As far as I am concerned, it is going to have to be pretty convincing evidence. I'd much rather we actually saw the leopard."

"What do we do if we do see it?" asked Nelson mildly. It appeared that Mr. Armand had hardly considered that possibility.

"If you boys see it, I certainly hope you'll call the rest of us, for I want one of my men to see it, at least. I don't think there's any danger, though. I think we can count on scaring it off with noise. Rather, it will probably leave when it hears us coming, long before any of us catches sight of it. I believe that's how a leopard acts in the movies—until it's cornered, at any rate." His tone had grown increasingly sarcastic, if not openly contemptuous.

Glancing backward as they left, Ted noticed a man run up to Mr. Armand, exchange a few sentences with him as though they were arguing, and then hurry off along the path at the edge of the lake. From his brief glimpse, Ted was unable to place him. Where had he come from and where was he going? There were only the two cars, so he hadn't come in that fashion, nor were there any boats drawn up along the edge of the lake as far as Ted could see. And either way around the lake, it was a long walk back to camp. Of course it was possible that the man had arranged for a boat to drop him and to pick him up later, but this still did not answer the question of what the man was doing there, at a time when Mr. Armand had claimed to be unable to raise additional manpower. Then Ted forgot all about the man in the excitement of the hunt.

Ted noticed that his position at the end of the line, toward the center of the woods and closer to the point where the tracks had been found, was perhaps a little more dangerous than the others. He had no one close at hand to help except Nelson, and it would take quite some time to assemble the others. As to the possibility of there being a leopard in the woods, he was of two minds, torn between practicality, and the mounting pile of evidence, including Holly's two stories. He decided that the best thing he could do would be to try to keep an open mind on the matter.

In spite of what Mr. Jackson had said, Ted believed that a leopard would be much more likely to hunt at night than in the daylight. Its big advantage would be its special cat eyes for seeing after dark, and it would probably also be afraid to be seen in the daylight. But if so, what would the leopard be likely to do in the daytime? Hole up in a cave? There didn't seem to be any. Then in a tree, perhaps? Here, too, the chances did not seem good, for the woods were hardly as thick as a jungle. They had few creepers or vines, and the foliage was thin enough to allow dapples of sunlight to penetrate to the forest path. Would these splotches of light, which so suggested the spots of a leopard, have led Holly to make a mistake?

So Ted found his excitement mounting, his senses keen and alert to every phase of the woods and the life it contained. He studied every overhanging limb as a possible hiding place, and watched for any traces on the path beneath his feet; he checked with Nelson, far on his left, from time to time; nor did he neglect the unpenetrated woods to his right. He did pick up a long pole and crash it into any suggestive-looking section of undergrowth. There was not a great deal of it, for this happened to be a branch of the state's well-kept park system. Still, a leopard would not need a great deal of underbrush to crouch beneath, waiting . . . waiting for what? Merely to lie unseen, or to leap out upon its unsuspecting prey, whether man or beast? Or was this all an empty danger, and they were merely frightening themselves like children telling ghost stories after dark?

And all the time Ted strained to hear those three blasts on a whistle which would mean danger and summon him to help. But the alarm never came. About fifteen or twenty minutes after the start, he heard the "census" whistles starting. He did not hear the first or the second, but thought he heard the third, and caught the others quite distinctly. After Nelson had blown seven times, he responded with eight. Then silence settled over the woods once more. They were all safe, they were still together, but he knew that none of the others had been more successful than himself. There were things to interest him, however. He noticed quite a number of strange and colorful birds, a few wild animals including a baby rabbit, numerous butterflies, and even a snake.

He had a slight fright when his way led him up a ravine, and to scramble out of it at the other end not only took a little time, but seemed to separate him from the others, so that for a few minutes he thought he had lost them.

He blew cautiously on his whistle eight times, hoping that Nelson would hear him but the others would not. Almost at once there were seven blasts, still to his left but in a slightly different direction than he had thought. He had to make double time for a while to regain his place in the line. Nelson gave him a wave as they came within sight of each other once more.

At regular intervals Mr. Armand started the signals going again. But at three-thirty there were three long blasts. Ted momentarily leaped to attention, thinking that this might be a signal the leopard had been sighted, but he immediately realized that this was merely an assembly call. They had reached the half way point of their expedition, and it was time to turn about and swing back. The whole excursion would take about four hours, and to ask half a dozen men to give up half a day's work apiece was a good deal. They could hardly expect Mr. Armand to do anything more than that for them.

"Well, I guess we've gone about as far as we can, or as far as necessary, for that matter," said Mr. Armand, when they had all assembled. "Up there ahead are open hills, and beyond them is a road, so I don't think there's much use going on. We'll just about get back for supper as it is, and I was hoping to get those fire-engine tracks cleared up before dark if I can, with Mr. Gordon coming back tomorrow. We'll take our horseshoe swing, then, and start back." He looked questioningly at the two boys, to see if they had any suggestions or criticisms to offer, but they were silent.

Being on the inside of the swing, Ted and Nelson had a little leisure while the men took their places in the new line. The men on the end did go a little way up the hill ahead, but not very far, not far enough to reach the top and look over, the boys observed. Then they made their wide swing and came down again. Well, if there was nothing but a road beyond there, what was the use?

"What do you think, Ted?" Nelson was walking slowly along toward his new position. "Is this the best way to hunt a leopard?"

"Do you know of any better way?" Ted returned.

"No, not unless you had about five thousand beaters the way they do in the movies."

"I don't think they have that many. They use the same ones over and over to make it seem like more."

"But the main question is, did we scour the woods thoroughly enough? Do you think a leopard would be more likely to take fright and dash off, or cower down and hide?"

"I don't know."

"And I don't either," said Nelson unnecessarily. "One thing is kind of funny, though. If you and I were the novices, why were we put on the end, and why didn't they separate us? Do you realize that on the way back we'll be very close to the same territory we explored before, while Mr. Armand will be near the other end, close to where the tracks were found?"

"Yes, I'd thought of that. But maybe Mr. Armand had his reasons. We're the novices, and he wanted more experienced men where he thought the greatest chance lay."

"Well, maybe," said Nelson skeptically, then hurried on ahead of Ted as the line was about ready to move.

The second part of the hunt was largely a repetition of the first, except that everyone was more tired and less excited and less alert. They hadn't seen a leopard before; why should they expect to see it now? Nor did they feel there was much chance of flushing it out ahead of them. If the leopard were going to run away, it was already high-tailing it in the opposite direction. But what would it do when it came to the road? Then it suddenly occurred to Ted that while Mr. Armand had said a road lay beyond the hills, he hadn't said how far. Maybe the woods still ran a good distance beyond; Ted wished now that he and Nelson had gone to the top of the hills to look. But maybe that was the way Mr. Armand had planned it, too. Anyway, what could they do, when the men clearly had to get back to camp, and even he and Nelson had no desire to get stranded out there after dark?

The whistle signals came at monotonously regular intervals, though they seemed longer than before. Nelson was hardly out of Ted's sight for more than a minute or two at a time, and no incidents occurred to delay the steady advance of the marchers. As five-thirty drew near, and Ted knew they were close to the lake, he realized the expedition had been a failure. Whether there was any leopard there to find remained an open question. This was the outcome that Mr. Armand had predicted, and Ted found himself reluctant to face the manager, who had fulfilled their request, but with a very poor grace.

However, there was no avoiding him, and when the group gathered again, Mr. Armand made no unusually sarcastic remarks, but merely instructed the men to get back to camp as quickly as they could. He hardly looked at the boys at all. The men, including Mr. Armand, set off at a steady walk, while Ted and Nelson followed at a more leisurely pace. With their own car available, there was no particular reason to hurry.

"Ted, have we been taken?"

"That's just what I'm trying to decide myself," said Ted slowly and thoughtfully. "Was Mr. Armand making a sincere effort to find that leopard, or wasn't he?"

"Maybe he was sincere enough in his own mind but didn't really believe there was a leopard. If so, he sure went to a lot of trouble just to keep a couple of newspaper cubs content and quiet. And there's still one thing that puzzles me. You could take me out in the woods and lose me by blindfolding me and turning me around three times. But I'm still willing to wager that nobody in the whole group got anywhere near the place where the leopard was supposed to have been seen and the tracks were found, or anywhere near that meadow Mr. Krause described, either."

"That's what I think, too. Of course, as Mr. Armand explained, a leopard would be sure to wander around a great deal, and we couldn't hope to cover the woods with a fine-tooth comb anyway. But this being true, where does it leave us?"

"You know very well where it leaves us," said Nelson. "It means that you and I are going to have to conduct our own search for that leopard. We'll be fewer in numbers, but we know more what we want and we can do just as we please. Think we ought to invite Gerald, too?"

"No, I guess not. I'd like to have him along, and he seemed disappointed to be left out. But if we start tampering with the other guests, Mr. Armand will have a genuine cause for complaint. Let's make it just you and me. We've worked through some tough situations in the past, and I don't think we're going to let a little old leopard stump us this time."

CHAPTER 8

THE TRAVELING MENAGERIE

Returning to camp, Ted and Nelson spotted Gerald and Holly, and went up to speak with them.

"Any luck with the leopard?" Gerald called, as soon as they were close enough to hear.

"Not so far," Nelson replied.

"Then does that mean I was wrong?" asked Holly, hardly knowing whether to be pleased or disappointed.

"We don't know that yet," Ted hastened to assure her. "We're not giving up on the leopard. We'll keep on looking for a while."

"Only of course there isn't any leopard," said Nelson to Ted as they walked on.

"How do you know that?"

"Because I know how people are. Oh, I don't mean *all* people are stupid, or even most people. The trouble is you never hear about the people who *didn't* see the leopard. But there are enough of the other kind to keep things boiling."

"And does that group include Holly?" asked Ted belligerently.

"Of course not. She's a sensible girl, and plays a fine game of tennis, and I'm sure she saw *something*. But a leopard—come on, now, Ted, we know she didn't see that. I'll bet you a nickel there isn't a leopard anywhere closer than the zoo in Weatherby."

But Ted did not feel like accepting even this modest wager.

Ted's exploit during the brush fire had spread through the camp, and a number of people who had not spoken to them before said hello to the boys as they passed. After supper, Jimmy's father came to their cottage to thank Ted.

"You sure made a good friend for life, Ted," Nelson said after he left. "And just for your own satisfaction, if you never did another useful thing in your life, you couldn't say your life was a failure."

Gerald led the others down to the tennis courts after supper, though they protested that it was too soon after eating. Fortunately they had to wait for an empty court. Nelson's game was showing improvement, and Gerald played with his usual finesse, so that the pair came out the winners, but Ted and Holly didn't mind.

"Seems too early for bed," said Nelson with a yawn, as the two boys walked home in the early twilight. "What do you feel like doing—checkers?" he suggested with a laugh, for this was a game he had no patience for.

"Why don't you concede five games to me, and then let's take a ride down to the village. I don't think I can sleep till I cool off, and anyway I'd like to telephone Mr. Dobson and let him know how things are coming along up here."

"What's wrong with the telephones at camp?"

"They all go through the switchboard at the business office, and it's possible that somebody might listen in. Since you and I both think Mr. Armand was leading us around by the nose today instead of making a sincere effort to find the leopard, let's keep him guessing about what we're going to do next."

"Good idea, Ted—especially since we don't know ourselves."

On the road to the village a surprise awaited them. At an exclamation from Ted, Nelson drew off to the side of the road and stopped. They stared up at a gaudy billboard advertisement: *HOLLAND'S TRAVELING MENAGERIE.*

"Set up at Crawford Corners," Nelson commented. "I'm glad you didn't take that bet of mine, Ted, because it looks like there is a leopard closer than Weatherby."

"Maybe not. They might not have a leopard with the show. I've always heard that a leopard is one of the most difficult animals to train. Besides, the show is just here this week, and if the leopard escaped from that show, it would have to be not later than last Sunday—"

"Now who said anything about a leopard escaping, Ted?" Nelson demanded, aggrievedly.

"Don't try to kid me, Nel. We still don't know whether there's a leopard on the loose, but if we're going to believe it, we have to find some explanation of where it came from. And I don't think it came from this show."

"But remember what Doctor Larken told us, Ted, about how a leopard that escaped from a *small* show might not be reported to the police. In spite of everything he said about a leopard traveling for a great distance through the woods without being detected, it would still be a lot easier for it to reach Vanishing Lake from Crawford Corners than from Weatherby or Alabaster. Crawford Corners is almost as far as Weatherby, but there're mostly woods in that direction."

"All well and good, Nel, provided we can prove that the show was in the neighborhood last week. I don't know how far ahead they would arrive, but it can't be very long, for a show like this can't afford to be idle."

"Well, why don't we take a ride up and see? You said you wanted to cool off."

"Tonight? It's thirty miles counting both ways, and if we do it, we'll be late getting back to camp and may have trouble getting in. No, I think it can wait for another day or two. But I would like to look in on the show soon. We may find out something about leopards, even if not about *our* leopard."

Nelson disclaimed any ownership, or even any real belief, in the Vanishing Lake leopard, but added, "Then just what is our schedule, Ted? I realize we're up here partly to work, but we still haven't been in that lake, and I've heard the fishing is awfully good, too. And besides, I haven't snapped a picture since those tracks last night."

"We're certainly going to work some of those things in, Nel. The leopard hunt isn't going to take all our time. But still, I think we ought to get up into that section of the woods we didn't see today, just as soon as we can. After that we'll play it by ear, but I'd like to visit the menagerie before the end of the week, if we can make it."

While Ted made his telephone call at the drugstore, Nelson looked over the selection of sports and photography magazines, and ended by purchasing half a dozen. They made the ten-o'clock closing time with a little to spare, and after locking up the car, Nelson went around the back to inspect his trunk compartment.

"What's the trouble?" asked Ted, following him around in the darkened parking lot.

"That darned door of mine keeps coming open and bouncing closed again. I want to make sure it's closed, even if I can't lock it."

"Nothing valuable in there, is there?"

"No, just a few tools and a spare tire that isn't as good as the ones I've got on, but I don't want to give the kids any ideas, either."

The door was indeed open a few inches, and Nelson slammed it shut. It was then that a plaintive sound came to their ears. They both listened, but it was not repeated.

"Sounded like a cat," said Nelson, puzzled, looking around him.

"And it sounded like it came from your luggage compartment," Ted added.

Nelson shook his head, but lifted the door again. Two gleaming eyes stared out at them.

"Careful," Ted warned, as Nelson reached in toward it, "it may be frightened."

Proceeding more cautiously while he uttered a few soothing words, Nelson grasped the animal and lifted it out gently, then put it upon his shoulder. The jet-black cat seemed satisfied to be there for the moment, and repeated its mewing sound.

"Hungry, probably," Nelson decided, snuggling the furry animal against his cheek. "I wasn't sure I liked cats, but this one seems friendly enough. It must have climbed in there while we were in the drugstore. Well, what do we do with it, Ted?"

"Take it with us to the cottage. What else can we do?"

"Remember that sign saying, 'Please do not bring pets to camp'?"

"I wouldn't say we brought this one, exactly. Anyway, we'll make sure it doesn't run around and bother the other guests."

"You mean," said Nelson as they started off toward their cottage, "it's all right to break a rule, as long as you don't get caught."

"That's not what I mean at all. I mean a rule has to be applied with common sense. I wouldn't ordinarily touch my neighbor's ladder without his permission, but if I needed it suddenly to rescue someone, I wouldn't wait around for permission. Common sense is the best rule of all."

It was late, and it was probable that no one would notice the black cat in the dark, but just the same they took the trail back of the cottages, where they were unlikely to run into anyone. They made the back door of their cottage without incident, and went inside. Nelson put the cat down in the middle of the floor, and they surveyed it critically. It didn't look particularly scrawny, but rather like someone's well-cared-for pet.

"How about getting it a dish of milk?" Nelson suggested, and when Ted had brought it, the cat settled down to drink it as if it belonged with them.

When Ted emerged from the bedroom in the morning, still stretching, he found Nelson on the floor of the kitchenette, playing with the black cat.

"Look at it, Ted," Nelson urged him, "this cat is as playful as a kitten. It'll snatch at things, go after a ball, and try to catch drops from the faucet. I didn't know a cat was this much fun."

"What did you give it to eat?" asked Ted, noticing the newly cleaned-out dish.

"Oh, I took an early run down to the store."

"Did they have cat food?"

"Don't be silly. I wouldn't have dared ask for it, even if they did. But I got a can of sardines, and this critter put away the whole thing and was looking around for more. I'll have to get some more, now that I know it likes them."

"You mean we're keeping the cat?" said Ted doubtfully. "You know, this is probably someone's pet. Why don't we take it back to the place near the drugstore where we parked, and let it go? It surely ought to be able to find its way home from there."

Nelson looked serious. "I've thought about that, Ted, and I'm not so sure that's were it belongs, after all. You know how my trunk door keeps popping open all the time. It might have climbed in almost anywhere."

"Where, for instance?"

"Well, maybe out there in the parking lot. This cat might be someone's pet right here at camp."

"You're not forgetting there's a rule against pets?"

"I know, but *we've* got a cat, haven't we, and nobody knows about it. Maybe somebody else had one, too."

Ted looked doubtful, and Nelson went on, "But it might have been somewhere else. We were up to Weatherby yesterday morning, and we made a couple of stops along the way. The cat may have been in the luggage compartment longer than we realize."

And Ted was forced to agree that this was so. Though the stop at the drugstore seemed to him the most likely one, he didn't like the idea of leaving the cat there, if it wasn't.

"Don't you think we ought to make some inquiries, Nel? Maybe there's some sort of humane society that could help us trace the owner, or find a new home for it."

Nelson grimaced. "I don't like that very much. You know what happens if they *don't* find a home for it, and I'm beginning to like this little thing. Besides, I think it likes me, too. Don't you think we could take it back to Forestdale with us?"

"And then what? My mother and I aren't home enough to take care of a pet properly. What about you?"

"I'd like it, all right, except that we've got a dog already, and that might lead to fireworks. But I'd be willing to try to find a home for it, and if I couldn't, then I could always turn it over to the humane society afterward."

"But first we're going to inquire, aren't we?"

"Oh, sure we are. I wouldn't like to take away somebody else's pet. But we don't have to do that right away, do we? Oh, Ted, I knew I had something else to tell you. When I was out to the store, I ran into Mr. Jackson. He told me that one of the twins was rushed to the hospital last night. And right now there's a car marked 'County Health Department' in the parking lot. I think they're going to test the water."

CHAPTER 9

THE WATER TEST

Ted wrinkled up his nose. "Going to test the water? What do you suppose that means?"

"Typhoid. That's what they usually test for, isn't it?"

"Yes, I guess so. And I suppose the story's all over camp by now."

"You bet. If Mr. Jackson knows it, it won't be long before everyone else does, too. Do you suppose a lot of people will pull out of camp right away?"

"I'll bet they're thinking of it, all right, and the only thing that's stopping them is that they aren't sure yet it's typhoid. But there's another angle to it, that if a general quarantine goes into effect, they might have trouble getting out. Mr. Armand certainly has his troubles."

"Well, what are you hanging around here for, Ted? Why don't you get out on your story?"

"What story? I came here to look for a leopard, not to worry about a typhoid epidemic."

"Does that mean you don't follow up a story that happens to get tossed in your lap? But of course if you're not interested, I can always call Ken Kutler," he concluded with a laugh, as he mentioned the name of the reporter from a rival paper.

Ted didn't need to be told where his duty lay, but this was a story for which he had a strong distaste. However, with his notebook and pencil ready, he started out for the office building. He took the more pleasant walk along the edge of the lake, and noted that it was going to be a fine day. Fishermen were out on the lake, and children were at play on the beach, among them one of the twins, looking a little lonely without his brother.

"Do you believe anybody could swim all the way across the lake?" he asked Ted.

"I imagine a good swimmer could—but don't you try it."

"I won't, 'cause I don't want to drown before Jeff comes home." He became confidential. "But I saw a man swim across the lake."

"Are you sure?" said Ted, narrowing his eyes. "That's against the rules."

"But it was at night, when nobody could see him."

"Then how did you see him?"

"I was looking out the window. I couldn't sleep because Jeff's throat hurt him. Then I saw this man out in the middle of the lake."

"Maybe he didn't swim all the way across. Maybe he was just out for a long swim."

The boy seemed willing to accept this idea, and upon further questioning wasn't even sure it was a man. It might have been a boat, for Ted supposed that the fishermen sometimes went out during the night.

At the parking lot he found the car Nelson had mentioned, and decided to wait there. That might be a little better than trying to talk with the man while other people were listening. Mr. Armand might even try to interfere with the interview, if he thought it would lead to unfavorable publicity for the camp. Ted did not have long to wait. A man soon emerged from the building and came toward the car. He had some small bottles in his hands, which Ted took to be samples of water.

Apparently the man realized that Ted was waiting for him, for he looked at him with some annoyance, noting the notebook and pencil.

"Are you a reporter?" he demanded.

"Yes. Ted Wilford of the Forestdale *Town Crier*."

"I've heard of it."

Ted wondered if he was supposed to feel flattered that the man had heard of the newspaper, but went on:

"Would you mind telling me why you are here this morning?"

"Certainly I would mind. I don't think it's any of your business."

"I thought that public health was everybody's business," Ted returned.

"I wouldn't know about that. The department pays my salary, and I do what I'm told, and that's all I've got to say about anything."

"Those look like water samples you're taking. Are you testing the water supply here?"

"You've got eyes in your head. You can see what you see, and draw your own conclusions."

"I don't think *Mr. Dobson* would care to print my conclusions."

The man's attitude changed at once.

"You are quite correct. These are water samples, and I am going to test the water for purity. But you would be completely wrong to draw any adverse conclusions from that. We make routine checks of the water at all camps, before the season starts, and then from time to time we make unscheduled spot checks."

"Is there any particular reason why a spot check was made here at this time?"

"I wouldn't care to say. I was told to come here, and I came."

"Would the fact that a boy was taken ill here yesterday have anything to do with it?"

"I told you that the department doesn't tell me its reasons."

"Are you testing the water for typhoid?" Ted asked directly.

"That, among other things. But I hope you won't use that word in print. It's a scare word, and we have no more reason to suspect typhoid than we do anything else."

"How long will it be before you know the water is pure?"

"Officially, the water is pure right now. But the tests may take a day or two. These things don't always come out on schedule. At that time I may find something to change the rating of the water, but the odds are strongly against it."

He nodded in a friendly way as Ted thanked him, and then drove off. But in spite of the man's reassuring words, Ted felt vaguely uneasy. Back at their cottage, he talked the matter over with Nelson.

"So it is typhoid, huh? I don't care much for that, but I don't believe in getting panicky about things, either. Why do they have to check the water here? Can't they check it where the water comes from?" Nelson asked.

"Maybe they want to be sure that the water coming out of the system is as pure as the water going into it." Ted considered. "I don't suppose the water comes from the lake, does it?"

"I don't think so, Ted. It probably comes from wells or springs."

"Well, what do we do now? We know the water is being tested for typhoid. Do we go on drinking it, just the way we did before?"

"Sure, we'll go on drinking it, Ted. You know what I think happened? I think the doctor is required to report any unusual illness to the health department, and under their regulations they have to test the water supply when such a report comes in, and it's all tied up in official red tape. If the health department thought there was any real danger, they would close down the supply. Anyway, what else can we do?"

"We could live on pop for a couple of days, I suppose, or get a water purifier from the drugstore, or boil our water for twenty minutes or half an hour."

"And then go around trying to catch the steam?" Nelson laughed, and Ted decided to laugh, too.

"I just thought of something," Nelson went on, not laughing now. "If the water supply is contaminated, the lake is probably worse, for it's probably fed from the same springs or wells. And I was looking forward to a good swim. We've been here for two days, and I haven't had a dip yet."

"You can swim with your head out of the water."

"If you can swim without splashing water in your face, you're a better swimmer than I am, and I don't think you are. Oh, the heck with it. I'm going in swimming the first chance I get. I'd even like to swim across the lake. I think I could do it."

"You'd better do more than think about it. You'd better be sure."

"Oh, I was going to have you along in a rowboat, in case I got a cramp or something. Nobody could stop us, if we started from the other side. What *are* we going to do today, Ted?"

"Leopard hunt—in the part of the woods that Mr. Armand seemed to be trying to steer us away from. All right by you?"

Nelson thought about it. "As right as it will ever be, I suppose. If there really is a leopard out there, I might as well get eaten up as the next person. I know you'll write a good story about me, and the wire services will gobble it up. I'll be famous—" But as he thought it over, he decided he wasn't that anxious to become famous.

Ted considered. If there really were a leopard at large, it would be advisable to organize a better expedition than they could manage alone. But it was impossible to organize such a leopard hunt at this stage, for hardly anyone really believed there was a leopard. He and Nelson ought to be willing to take some risk to run the story to earth.

The threat could only be ended by either proving the story wrong, or capturing the creature.

"Take your fishing pole along," Ted directed, as they made ready to leave.

Nelson looked at his friend as though he doubted his sanity for a moment. "A fishing pole?" he repeated.

"Sure. We're going out fishing, and we'll just sort of drift across the lake. There's no use telling everybody what we're up to."

The cat was shut in the kitchenette with food and water. Nelson gave the pet a few affectionate strokes in parting, and the cat responded by rubbing against him and purring contentedly.

On the way to the lake, the boys ran into Gerald and Holly, but Gerald did not invite them to play tennis, since it was apparent from the fishing pole that they had other plans.

"Well, I hope the fish bite," Gerald called to them. "Look us up later if you feel like tennis. You'll know where to find us," and of course they did. Gerald wouldn't be very far from the tennis courts if he could help it.

The man at the pier helped them with their boat, and supplied a can of live bait, which Nelson had forgotten about. He even offered to loan a fishing pole to Ted, but the latter declined on the grounds that he would be busy enough handling the oars. As a final piece of advice, the man suggested the far corner of the lake as a desirable spot, which fortunately was in the direction they planned to go anyway.

They started off, Ted rowing easily. Nelson soon had his line trailing in the water, but there was no bait on his hook, for he didn't care to catch anything just then.

"Ted!" Nelson said suddenly.

"What?"

"Don't turn around now, but remember that little bridge at the head of the lake, that we crossed in the car yesterday afternoon?"

"Sure."

"Well, when you get a chance, take a casual look over there and see what you see."

Ted managed it within a minute or so, and without staring, remarked to Nelson, "Just a man standing on the bridge, as far as I can tell."

"Sure, just a man, but do you know what he's holding in his hands? A pair of binoculars."

"Well, I don't suppose there's any law against that."

"No, but he seemed particularly interested in what we were doing, for he put them down quickly when he saw me glance that way. Do you know who he is?"

"No, and you don't either. We're too far away to tell."

"Want to take a row over and see?"

"No, what's the use? If he didn't want us to see him, he'd just casually stroll off before we could get much closer."

"Then what are you doing?"

"Nothing, just turning the boat a little, and you may as well put some real bait on your hook, because the leopard hunt's off. We'll go sometime when we can sneak away. I've got a feeling we'll have a better chance of discovering what's going on around here if nobody else knows what we're up to."

CHAPTER 10

THE SPOTTED CAT

The fish Nelson caught were too small to win any prizes, but big enough to keep, and when he had landed three, he decided, reluctantly, to call it a morning.

"That's one for each of us, Ted"—he was of course including the cat—"and if I take any more they may go to waste. Besides, I just remembered I'm going to have to clean these myself."

It occurred to Ted that if the lake was polluted, the fish might be contaminated, too. But if you went on thinking this way, pretty soon you would be afraid of everything. He decided to say nothing about the possibility, remote in any case.

On shore, they fell into step with Gerald and Holly once again. Remembering the man on the bridge, Ted asked if they had happened to notice him.

"No, I'm afraid not," Holly admitted. "But if you're really interested, why not ask Mr. Jackson? He seems to know just about everything that's going on around here."

"How could I ask him? I don't have much of a description of the man."

"You said he was carrying binoculars. That ought to be enough for Mr. Jackson. There probably aren't very many of these in camp."

She did not pry further, assuming that Ted, as a newspaper reporter, might have business which he did not care to discuss with her. Meanwhile, Gerald, who had been walking with Nelson, was impatient. He had asked Nelson to play tennis that afternoon, and Nelson had replied he was going to swim. Gerald now raised his voice so that Ted and Holly could also hear.

"You don't mean that you're going swimming in that lake, when it might have typhoid bacteria in it?"

Over his shoulder Nelson exchanged a quick glance with Ted. Their supposition that Mr. Jackson had spread the story around was right.

"What's this about typhoid?" asked Nelson, playing it dumb.

"Why, sure, didn't you know they're testing the water for typhoid? Holly and I aren't drinking any water today, and we aren't going into the lake either. Typhoid fever is nothing to fool around with."

"Oh, I think it's all perfectly silly," Holly interposed. "I'm sure there isn't any typhoid here. It's just one of those stories which go around. Nobody knows how they get started, and there's no way of stopping them because you can't actually disprove them."

"Whom did you hear the story from—Mr. Jackson?" Ted inquired.

"No, I don't think so. As a matter of fact, several people mentioned it to us. But for all I know, *they* may have gotten the story from Mr. Jackson."

Ted looked down at the beach. There did seem to be fewer bathers than usual, and some of the children were avoiding the water, as though they had been forbidden to go in. What would all of this do to the camp and the vacation season? If it was Mr. Jackson's work, Ted felt that he was behaving in an extremely irresponsible fashion.

"I wonder why Mr. Armand doesn't do something about Mr. Jackson's tongue?" he speculated.

"Just how do you go about stopping a guest's tongue?" Nelson demanded.

"Oh, I don't think it's Mr. Armand's problem—not any more," said Holly quickly. "I understand Mr. Gordon is due back this afternoon, and probably Mr. Armand will turn the whole thing over to him. We've met Mr. Gordon before, and he's a wonderful man. You'll like him, Ted."

They came to a stop near the Jergens' cottage, Gerald still pressing for a tennis date, and finally Nelson agreed to play at one o'clock.

"I was afraid he'd keep arguing till we got back to our own cottage," Nelson explained to Ted, "and then he might hear our cat mewing. You didn't mind, did you, Ted?"

"Oh, no, I guess we'll have time for a little tennis. Then I'd like to do the same thing we planned this morning—try to drift across the lake without attracting any particular notice and see what we can find in the woods. If we get back in time we may run up to that traveling menagerie tonight."

"To see if a leopard escaped?"

Ted grinned. "To see a lot of things."

Their cat was glad to see them, and Nelson tossed it a few choice tidbits—saving the fish for later.

"I'd like to take it out for a little romp," Nelson decided. "There's a little glade out in the woods, where I had it out this morning. Nobody saw us."

"But it's later now. Some of the children, especially, may be running around."

"Let them see it. It's just a little cat. Unless somebody complains to Mr. Armand, it won't matter. And I don't even care about him. Maybe he'll say I've got to get rid of the cat or leave camp. And I'll say my friend Ted Wilford of the *Town Crier* won't write a very good story about him. And he'll say—"

"He probably won't say anything. It'll be up to Mr. Gordon. But take the cat out, if you want to, and I'll cook lunch."

Ted had bacon frying on the stove in a few minutes, but it was still half cooked when Nelson came tearing back to the cottage.

"Ted! Ted! Come here, quick!"

"What's the matter? Where's the cat?" Ted shut off the burner, and dashed out after his friend.

"The cat's all right. I left it out in the glade." Though excited, Nelson kept his voice down to avoid attracting attention. Fortunately the near-by cottages were vacant. "But, Ted, I want to show you something. This cat's got spots!"

"What kind of spots?"

"*Black* spots."

"You're crazy. How could a black cat have black spots?"

"It does, though. You'll see."

They came upon the cat in the glade, playing lazily in the sun. Nelson had had no fear of its wandering off. It seemed too tame, too playful, and strangely enough, too *young*. Then Ted saw that Nelson had indeed been right. Black spots showed on the animal that had not been visible in a weaker light. Either the spots were a different shade of black, or were more glossy, for in the bright sunlight they showed distinctly, making an interesting pattern—a pattern they had seen before only on a much more fearsome animal.

Ted's first impulse was toward caution. "It has black spots, all right, but that may not mean anything. Remember, there are some cats that have stripes like a tiger. Maybe this is just one of those things."

"But that's not all, Ted. Those teeth and those claws are pretty sharp already. I've picked up a few scratches, and it's nipped at my clothes a little. You expect that kind of behavior from a kitten or a puppy, but when an animal gets full grown it usually becomes a little more dignified. But this one still acts like a baby. Ted, is there such a thing as a *black* leopard?"

"I—I don't know. I've got sort of a hazy recollection that there is. I don't believe I have ever seen one."

"And I've never seen a baby leopard, either. How do we know but maybe they're black when they're little and turn yellow later?"

But Ted shook his head in disagreement. "I don't think anything this black is ever going to turn yellow. But those spots—I know where we can get some quick information about it, though. I'll call Doctor Larken at the zoo. He'll know."

"But what'll you tell him, Ted?"

"Oh, I won't tell him about this—this cat. I'll just ask a few questions. If he tries to question me, I can always say I'm protecting my source."

"And we're going to need some protecting, Ted. If we thought it was important to keep a cat hidden, it's all the more important to hide a baby leopard, if that's what it is."

He picked the cat up and put it gingerly on his shoulder. Just ten minutes before he had been playing quite carelessly with the animal. But it was one thing to play with a domestic cat, and quite another to play with an animal you knew would soon be too large and too dangerous to be handled so casually. But though Nelson's feelings had changed, the cat's had not, and it rode along quite contentedly. The boys hurried into the cottage, and Nelson put the cat down on the floor and regarded it with a frown.

"And I thought we were going to be buddies," he muttered. "But I can see *that's* not going on very long." Then he relented a little, and scratched the animal under the chin. It *was* a cute pet, no matter what it really was or how soon it would stop being cute and become dangerous.

Ted decided to give up on the bacon. It was burned in some parts, and undercooked in others, but they made sandwiches, and Nelson tossed a section of bacon to the cat. It leaped at the food—was it only their imaginations again?—with a ferocity unusual in a domesticated animal, and its eyes seemed to gleam like those of the jungle hunter.

"I wonder how old it is?" said Nelson, watching the creature through narrowed eyes. "It certainly isn't as big as the cubs we saw at the zoo."

"No, but since a lion is a little larger than a leopard, I imagine the cubs would also be a little larger at a similar age."

"But those cubs were still with their mama," Nelson pointed out. "If this one is the same age, it can't be very long away from its mother, either."

"I know. That's what I was thinking."

"Well, then, where is its mother? Is she out there somewhere in the woods? But the leopard Holly reported seeing was spotted, and this one is black. Then that couldn't be the mother, could it?"

"I don't know about that. But it still makes me wonder how this cat got in your trunk compartment. Do you still think it happened in the parking lot, or in front of the drugstore, or on the road to Weatherby?"

"No, Ted, I don't. I think it happened right out there in the woods. Remember my car was parked there for several hours."

"But could it have gotten in by itself?"

"It might have. My trunk compartment pops open whenever I hit a hard bump, and goodness knows that road around the lake had enough bumps. I suppose the cat might have gotten lost, and thought that was a good place to hole up in. Poor thing, we didn't find it till late last night, and we might not have found it till today, if we hadn't just happened to hear it purring."

They finished eating quickly because Ted was anxious to phone Dr. Larken, doing so from the village to avoid any eavesdroppers in the camp office. But they were faced with the problem of what to do with the cat in their absence.

"I don't think we can get it to the car without someone noticing," Ted observed. "Anyway, I think it'll be all right here. No one has discovered it so far as we know."

Nelson was less willing to leave the cat now, being convinced that a baby leopard was not as able to take care of itself as a full-grown domestic cat. But he finally agreed with Ted that the best thing to do was to leave it.

"What about the office, Ted? They have their own keys to this place, don't they? I don't suppose there's anything to stop Mr. Armand from walking right in if he wants to, is there? And I suppose they do send cleaning women around once in a while."

"We're only here for a week. I don't think anyone will be coming in here till we're gone—unless Mr. Armand is suspicious, and our job is to keep him from being suspicious. We'll lock it up in the kitchenette, and hope it doesn't get to raising a fuss that will attract attention."

Ted pulled down the shade over the window in the back door. He was about to pull down the other shades, too, but Nelson stopped him.

"That will look too suspicious, Ted, as though there were some funny business going on. But I think we can arrange the curtains so that it will be hard for anyone to see in, especially in the daylight."

After doing this, they decided they had covered matters as well as they could. "Unless it decides to go on a rampage," said Nelson gloomily. "If regular cats do that sometimes, what could a baby leopard do if it made up its mind?"

They left nothing on the table or sink to attract the cat, and it seemed contented enough as they departed. They were soon in the village, and Ted got Dr. Larken on the line.

"Doctor Larken, this is Ted Wilford of the Forestdale *Town Crier*. Remember me?"

"Of course I do, Wilford. What can I do for you? Any more news about that leopard of yours?"

"Not exactly, but I have a couple of questions. Is there such a thing as a black leopard?"

"Oh, I see. Your witness isn't so sure about the spots. Is that your difficulty?"

"Let's just call it a hypothetical question," said Ted cautiously.

"All right, Wilford, I'll play along. Yes, there is a black leopard. In some areas of the world it's just as common as the better-known spotted leopard."

"Would it be possible for a spotted leopard to have a black cub?"

"Oh, my, yes, that's quite ordinary. As a matter of fact, there may be both spotted and black cubs in the same litter."

"Now, could one of these black cubs have black spots like the spotted leopard, spots that could only be seen in a bright light?"

"It might, Wilford. I'm not certain that it happens in all cases, but it certainly does in some. I take it that your interest in a baby leopard is due to the fact that your witness isn't so sure about the size any more. Maybe you're going to end up with a lynx after all, Wilford."

"Maybe," said Ted noncommittally.

"Then you don't have any more information for me, something that would justify my taking a day off and coming up your way?" The doctor sounded disappointed.

"Afraid not. We hope to go out into the woods again this afternoon for another look."

"Well, happy hunting."

"Thank you, and I appreciate your help. I'll call you if I do come up with anything."

Ted relayed all this information to Nelson, and they stared at each other in silence for some moments.

"I guess there's no question that it really is a leopard, then," Nelson decided.

"That's the way I see it. And now the big question is: what do we do next?"

CHAPTER 11

MR. JACKSON'S GOSSIP

The discovery of the nature of their cat made some of their other plans even more imperative.

"I think we'd better hunt for that leopard in the woods just as soon as possible, Ted," said Nelson thoughtfully. "If it really is the mother, we ought to return her cub as fast as we can. But I admit I don't want to be the one to hand over the cub to her and say, 'Sorry, it was all a mistake.' Another thing, Ted, is, why are some leopards black and some spotted? I should think a spotted leopard would make a better daytime hunter, because its coat would blend into the leaves and grass in the bright light, while a black leopard would make a better night hunter. And since the one we're hunting is spotted, I'm not so keen about going in the daytime. Guess we'll have to, though. We could never find it at night."

While admitting that there might be a little something in Nelson's theory, Ted agreed they would have to go in the daylight.

"Maybe it would be better if we could organize a real expedition," he decided, frowning.

"But whom could we get?" Nelson inquired. "Mr. Armand and his crew certainly won't go out again. You admit you don't have enough evidence to ask Doctor Larken to come over. I'm afraid the police would laugh at you. And if we tried to get a group of campers together, I think about half the campers would decide to leave instead of joining us on the hunt, and we would be doing the very thing we've been criticizing Mr. Jackson for."

"And the main objection is that I believe we'd diminish our chances of really finding out what is going on. We've got to move as cautiously and as secretly as possible. If anybody does find out what we're up to, we're going to have to do some tall explaining about that leopard cub in our cottage."

"But we haven't done anything wrong," Nelson reminded him.

"Maybe not, but sometimes you have to do a lot of explaining to prove it. And after all, I am down here on a newspaper assignment, and the most important thing to do is to run down the story in the best way I can. Another thing I want to do is to get up to that traveling menagerie tonight if we possibly can. Now that we know we've got a baby leopard on our hands, maybe we can get some information on how to take care of it, and decide what we're going to do with it eventually."

"A baby leopard ought to have some value, shouldn't it, Ted? I don't mean we'll get rich with a reward, or anything like that, but a zoo or a circus ought to be glad to have it."

"Well, we'll have to see about it. For all we know this leopard may belong to someone who is anxious to get it back. It may simply have been lost, strayed, or stolen."

"Mama leopard, too?" said Nelson skeptically. "And I'm not convinced that the baby didn't get into my trunk compartment with a little outside help. Say, maybe the thief stowed it there because the mother leopard was chasing him and—"

"—and caught him," Ted finished gruesomely. They both laughed, but it wasn't exactly a laughing matter when they considered that they themselves would be out in the woods that afternoon looking for the leopard.

Reaching their cottage, they found the black cub safe and lively, and pleased to see Nelson again. They almost regretted their tennis date with the Jergenses, but there seemed no help for it. Certainly they could not hope to slip unseen and un-missed across the lake if they were supposed to be playing tennis.

After a few sets, they stopped to rest. Suddenly Holly noticed a man approaching them, and waved to him.

"That's Mr. Gordon, Ted," she said. "Come along and I'll introduce you."

She did so, and the camp owner shook hands warmly with Ted.

"You must be that young newspaper reporter Mr. Armand was telling me about. Well, I don't expect you to write anything except the truth, but we'll try to make the truth pleasant by making your stay here just as pleasant as possible. Is there anything I can do for you?"

"No, I don't think so, unless you'd care to answer a couple of questions. What's the truth about this typhoid business?"

"There is no typhoid here," said Mr. Gordon seriously. "If I thought there was the slightest indication of it, I'd immediately close down the beach and ship in bottled water. I imagine that their mother got excited over the illness of one of her twins, called up the health board, and requested a check on the water. I'm certain that someone called, but of course they won't tell me who it was."

"Do you intend to do anything about it at all?"

"I've instructed Mr. Armand to keep in touch with the health department, and as soon as their report is ready, I'm going to have notices posted, signed by the health department, certifying that the water is O.K."

"What about the leopard in the woods?"

"Let's be sensible about that, Ted. Of course there's no leopard anywhere around here. I've gone into the matter very thoroughly with Mr. Armand, and he explained to me just how the story began. I believe there is only one person who claims to have seen the leopard, and I suppose that was someone who is very excitable and has a good imagination." Evidently he was not aware Holly was the person whose story was chiefly responsible for the leopard scare. Holly did nothing to enlighten him.

"Unfortunately," Mr. Gordon concluded, "it would be much easier to prove there *is* a leopard, if there really is one, than it would be to prove there *isn't* a leopard. I don't know any way to go about that except to use ordinary common sense."

After general farewells, Ted and Nelson started off. As soon as they were out of earshot of their friends, Nelson remarked:

"Well, I think we've escaped from the Jergenses for the time being. All ready to slip across the lake? You mosey down to the pier and get a boat ready, and I'll go back to the cottage for my fishing pole. Great Caesar's ghost, here comes Mr. Jackson. Try to shake him, Ted, before I get back."

Mr. Jackson came up to Ted as Nelson left and greeted him warmly. "Haven't seen much of you for a while, Ted. How's everything going?"

"Well enough."

"Nothing new on the leopard?"

"Nothing to put in the paper. You heard about the hunt Mr. Armand staged yesterday, but we didn't find anything."

"But you're not going to give up, are you?" asked Mr. Jackson in disappointment.

"What else can I do? I can't seem to pick up any reliable evidence, and I only have a few days left. My boss instructed me to have a little fun on this trip, and Mr. Gordon has announced a new fishing competition, so we've decided to enter."

Mr. Jackson leaned forward confidentially. "Didn't you hear about what happened at the Kyloe farm? You should have. You saw Mr. Kyloe in the woods yesterday when you were hunting for the leopard. He was the man who was having the argument with Mr. Armand."

"How do you know all that?" asked Ted in amazement.

The elderly man looked mysterious. "Oh, I have ways of finding out things. Not to mention any names, but I'm on good terms with some of the employees, and they tell me things."

"What were they arguing about?" Ted demanded.

"Oh, I can tell you that, too. One of Mr. Kyloe's calves was slain the previous night—by the leopard, he claims."

"And he's blaming Mr. Armand for that?"

"I don't know who he's blaming, but he doesn't want it to happen again. Now do you believe there's a leopard in the woods? You'll have to excuse me now, Ted. I see Mr. Gordon over there, and I want to tell him something."

With a cordial wave of his arm, Mr. Jackson strode off with a sprightliness which denied his advanced years. Ted wondered if his story could be true. He seemed to have produced it just as Ted gave signs of giving up on the leopard hunt. On the other hand, he was certainly right about Mr. Kyloe and Mr. Armand having an argument out in the woods. Maybe he was right about the rest of it, too.

Nelson was soon back with his pole and bait, and they started across the lake with Ted at the oars as before. This time he did not head toward the spot on the opposite shore where they intended beginning to explore, but to a point farther down the lake, near where their car had been parked. Later, when they were on the other side, they could row up to the proper place, hoping that by then any observers on the home shore would have grown disinterested or lost them among the other boats on the lake. The person they were most afraid of was Mr. Jackson, but they saw him engaged in earnest conversation with Mr. Gordon, and then the two of them started off somewhere. It was apparent that they had other things on their minds.

The row across the lake took much longer than it did the first time they crossed with Mr. Jackson and headed directly for the place they intended to land. As far as Ted could tell, no one seemed to be watching them or paying much attention to them at all. However, he continued the same cautious pace, just as though, Nelson exclaimed sarcastically, he wasn't very anxious to meet up with the leopard.

But they started along the far shore at last, finally reaching the spot where they had originally landed with Mr. Jackson. It was then that they noticed another rowboat drawn up upon the shore.

"I wonder if that means we've got to call things off once more," said Nelson in disgust.

Before Ted could reply, two young boys dashed out of the woods.

"Hey, hey!" one boy called, but that apparently exhausted his efforts, and it was up to the other boy to explain.

"We just saw the leopard—back there in the woods!"

CHAPTER 12

"SOMETHING"

Ted and Nelson waited until the two younger boys had partly recovered. They soon calmed down enough to tell their story.

"We went off in the woods," the larger boy explained, "because we wanted to collect leaves for our nature collection, and then all at once we saw the leopard sitting on the path watching us. It had a great big tongue and it was licking around the side of its mouth. Then I said to Cortland, 'Hey, Cortie, there's the leopard,' and he said, 'Let's beat it out of here fast,' and we turned around and ran. Then we saw you, and we screamed. We thought maybe you were just leaving, and we didn't want you to go off without us." This rather long recital, in addition to his excitement, left him quite breathless.

Ted questioned him closely. "Are you sure it was a leopard?"

"Yes, I'm sure. I saw one like it in the zoo one time."

"What about you, Cortland, did you see the leopard, too?"

The smaller boy's eyes were as big as saucers as he nodded his head affirmatively.

"If you're going to catch it you'd better hurry up," said the other boy impatiently. "Maybe it's still there." He seemed to believe that Ted and Nelson were not afraid, but anxious to capture the beast.

"All right, we'll try it," Nelson assured him. "Now get on your way. Did you row all the way across the lake?"

"No, only from the Point. There's a bunch of us there with our counselor."

"Well, you get back there as quickly as you can and tell your counselor exactly what happened. Get in and I'll shove you off—and don't go near the dam."

The boy gave him a scornful look to show that he knew better than that, but he and his friend scrambled into the boat. He picked up the oars, and after getting a push from Nelson started rowing as fast as he could.

"Well, let's go," Nelson ordered. "No use waiting for reinforcements. We don't know whether anyone else will be coming, and the animal might be gone by that time anyway. It didn't sound too dangerous, if it was just sitting there on the path, and maybe we'll find out it's only a bobcat after all."

He started off into the woods. Ted looked around for a possible weapon. The oars of the boat were somehow locked in place and he didn't have time to figure out how to get them off. Anyway, an oar would probably be too bulky, and the same went for the fishing pole, which was too flimsy besides. But he did pick up his tennis racket, thinking perhaps he could throw it at the beast if necessary and frighten it away. Then he set off at a slow jog, soon overtaking Nelson.

Nelson was all eyes as he stalked ahead, his glance, never still for a moment, jumping from side to side, from limbs to earth. Presently he discovered a print in the dust of the path, and pointed it out to Ted.

"What do you think now, Ted?"

"Well, it's a print of something, all right, but it's not distinct enough to tell."

"Yes, I thought for a moment maybe those boys were just scaring themselves, but they surely must have seen something. That stirred up spot may be the place where it was sitting down. Chances are it took off again as soon as it saw the boys, but they didn't wait long enough to see it. Well, how does a leopard run away? Does it leap for a tree, does it follow a path, or does it head cross country in a straight line?"

Ted had no better idea than he did, so they continued to follow the path ahead and hope for further tracks. In this they seemed doomed to disappointment, however, for unlike the flaked mud where they had found the track, the rest of the path was high, dry, and partly overgrown with weeds. From time to time they paused to listen, hoping that the leopard, if it really was such a huge beast, might be heard crashing through the underbrush, but there were no sounds except the normal noises of the summer woods.

They soon reached a fork in the path, and had to make up their minds which one to follow. At the junction they made a careful search for further indications, but found nothing. They would have to decide on pure intuition.

"We might as well go this way," Nelson indicated, pointing to his right. "That will take us into the part where we intended to go anyway, before we saw the boys. The other path will lead us into the section that Mr. Armand and his men explored yesterday. Or do you think it might be better to separate?"

"Nothing doing," said Ted shortly. The two of them together might cope with as powerful an enemy as a leopard, but separately it might be fatal.

Nelson turned down the path to the right, Ted at his heels still carrying the ridiculous tennis racket. Did anybody ever go hunting for a leopard with a tennis racket?

But Nelson proceeded indomitably, with Ted his willing follower. Ted had no idea what was going on in Nelson's mind, but surely he must have recognized the danger involved in meeting a leopard in the woods, even, perhaps, a partly tamed leopard escaped from a circus or a zoo. An escaped creature would certainly be frightened, and who could tell what a frightened leopard might do? Maybe Nelson's courage was based upon a strong disbelief that there was such an animal. But Ted didn't think so. Though Nelson didn't know whether there was a leopard or not, he was going ahead just the same. It represented a challenge to him and he was eager to meet it.

Nor was Ted quite certain of his own feelings. This had started out as a newspaper assignment, of course, but devotion to his profession didn't require him to risk his life. Yet here he was following a path which might lead them into deadly peril. Would he have gone even if Nelson hadn't been there? Yes, Ted thought probably he would, but a little more slowly and cautiously, a little less confidently. What was leading him on? Curiosity? Yes, partly that, an eagerness to unravel a difficult problem. But it was something else, too—an acceptance of a responsibility.

As they advanced along the path, they found the tension which had gripped them gradually relaxing. So far there was no sign of the leopard, and there seemed to be less likelihood now that they would run into it. They had a starting point, true enough, but imagining this point as the center of a semicircle, and the leopard bounding away from it in a straight line, the chance that they had chosen the right direction and would come upon the beast was growing ever less.

"I'm beginning to think I'm going to feel very silly if there *isn't* a leopard." Nelson scowled.

"Why feel silly?" Ted retorted. "Do firemen feel silly when they go out on a false alarm? They showed they were willing to meet whatever danger came their way. What more can you expect of them?"

"Just the same, I hope the fellows at home don't hear about it."

"They won't unless you tell them," Ted replied, but he had very little faith in Nelson's ability to keep his mouth closed.

"You know what I'm thinking though, Ted? Look how big these woods are, and how difficult it is for us to find a leopard that's supposed to be here. Then think about Mr. Jackson. After Holly's scare, he was able to go right out in the woods and find the leopard tracks. What do you think about that?"

"Pretty remarkable."

"It's more than remarkable for a man that's about eighty years old. I'm thinking that either he knew right where those tracks were, or else he made them himself. Would you have been able to find those tracks again, after he showed them to us?"

"No, I don't think so—not without a great deal of trouble. But maybe he's more familiar with these woods than we are."

"Familiar? You think a man his age makes a practice of prowling through these woods until he knows every path? That's a job for kids. And anyway I think Mr. Jackson's got better things to do—like getting people to listen to him."

This section of the woods was similar to the section they had explored with Mr. Armand the preceding day, with the exception that it led to higher ground. A half mile of winding trail eventually brought them to a grass plateau, which was probably where Mr. Krause, out with his son and another boy, had noticed the waving grass. Some of their tension returned as they realized this might be the leopard's regular stalking grounds.

"I've heard leopards sometimes like open ground," Nelson remarked, studying the tall blades of grass which were rustling slightly from the wind but apparently from nothing else. "Want to cross it, Ted?"

Ted considered. It was quite a long distance across the field. The leopard certainly wasn't there now, unless it was crouched and hiding, and then they weren't likely to find it—unless it decided to attack. The field was either dangerous or useless.

"No, let's keep on along the path and see where it leads. It's kind of worn down, and I'm wondering just why it should be. You wouldn't think there would be many hikers out this far in the woods."

The path circled a corner of the field, and they plunged into the woods again. The path began to rise once more, and the woods were broken by small ravines.

"Careful," Nelson cautioned. "Whatever you do, don't get that leopard boxed up in a corner. Always leave it a way out. If it thinks it's cornered, it could get really nasty."

The trail now led them into one of these ravines, about twice the height of their heads, and not a great deal wider. The ravine, deepening slightly, took several turnings, before suddenly widening out. And there, to their surprise, they came across a cabin in a clearing. Somehow it had never occurred to them that there might be houses in these woods. Even if these were public lands, this might be the home of some ranger or keeper who was permitted to live there.

"Can't tell if it's abandoned," Nelson observed. "Somebody may live here."

There were shades on the windows, and even from a distance they could see some sort of furniture within.

"If anyone lives there, I hope he enjoys having a leopard for a neighbor," Ted remarked.

Since it might be someone's home, they could not simply enter uninvited. Etiquette, if not law, required them to knock upon the door. They did so, but there was no response. Nelson shrugged.

"Want to go on, Ted?"

"Sure, why not? We might as well see this thing through."

"O.K., but I've about given up on the leopard. If somebody is really living in that cabin, it means that either there's no leopard, or else he knows a good deal more about it than we do."

They took to the trail once more. Unconsciously they found their vigilance relaxed, as the path took a turn, and there, sitting on the trail a hundred feet ahead of them—

"Ted! Ted!" Nelson's voice was low and urgent. "There it is! It's the leopard!"

"Where?" Ted demanded, for Nelson's bulky form was blocking his vision.

"Never mind now. Get back, back." He waved his arms desperately.

"Back to where?"

"To the cabin. Maybe we can get in. That'll be the safest place."

Still keeping himself between Ted and the animal, Nelson practically pushed him along the path and around the turn. Then side by side they set off at a swift trot for the cabin. Maybe this wasn't the smartest thing to do; they had heard that it is the nature of a hunting beast to pursue a running object. But they had no time to be smart. That cabin was close at hand, and represented a good refuge, if they could reach it and get in.

Reach it they did, in a matter of seconds that afterward seemed to be long minutes. Nelson put his hand on the knob, rattled it, and the door opened. They pushed in, banging the door closed behind them. Nelson found a back door ajar, and slammed that, too. Then at last they could take a deep breath.

"So there really is a leopard!" Ted exclaimed.

"You bet your sweet life there is. I saw it just as clear as daylight."

"What did it look like?"

"A great big cat with spots, sitting in the middle of the path, licking its whiskers. What more do you want?"

Ted felt that he had already had much more than he wanted. He would much have preferred to be able to prove the leopard wasn't there. He had changed his mind so often, he no longer was certain whether he had believed in the leopard or not. Holly could have been just a stage-struck girl wanting publicity; Mr. Jackson may have been pursuing his own devious purposes; the waving grass might have been a freak of the wind; the two boys could have been hysterical. Maybe Nelson, too, was merely the victim of an optical illusion. So far Ted himself had not seen the leopard. But no, if Nelson—a reasonable and hard-minded friend—had seen it, it had to be there. Ted walked over to a window to try to catch a glimpse of it himself.

Peer out as he might, he was unsuccessful. Of course it was possible that the leopard had made no attempt to follow them. They had not waited to see what it did. Maybe they had scared it as much as it had scared them.

Ted turned away from the window, letting the shade fall back into place, and at that moment there was a heavy thud on the roof. A large animal had leaped upon it and they could hear claws tearing at the shingles, mixed with unmistakable feline sounds of impatience.

CHAPTER 13

THE CAT ON THE ROOF

There was no doubt that the big cat knew they were inside; that was the reason for its almost frenzied attack upon the roof. How strong was that roof anyway? The boys didn't know, though the rest of the cabin seemed substantial. But what if the cat could tear a hole and drop through to the room below; what would they do then?

"I know one thing," said Nelson firmly. "I won't be anywhere around to find out. When the leopard comes in, I'm going out."

That was probably the best answer. If the creature did get in, and they were outside with the door closed, it might have more difficulty getting out of the cabin than it did in. Or what about the windows? An animal of this size would probably be capable of shattering them, but would it do it? Would it know enough, would it be fearless enough?

"Listen!" Ted ordered. They were silent for a moment. "It's moving about, trying another spot. That must mean it isn't making very much headway. I don't think it's going to make it."

"Unless it finds a loose shingle somewhere," Nelson responded. However, they both felt a little encouraged, and Nelson moved a little distance away from the door, where he had been standing ready to throw it open and dash out.

"I'm not sure about those windows, though," said Ted, pondering. "If it decided it can't get in through the roof, it might try one of those. Then what do we do?"

"Run into the bedroom and barricade the door." The cabin was divided into a living room and a bedroom. "But I don't know how long that flimsy door would hold an angry leopard, either."

They could not expect to hide from it in the bedroom for long. Its acute hearing and sense of smell would detect their presence. Still, the bedroom seemed the only possible retreat, in case the cat did break in through a window, and outside flight would be useless.

Cats, even big cats, can move very quietly, but its weight was evident as it climbed across the roof, and every step resounded in the room below. Then suddenly the cat gave a great leap to the ground and dashed off. Ted caught a fleeting glimpse of it through the window. The size, the spots, the tail were unmistakable.

"Well, now, you've seen it, too, Ted."

"Yes—I saw it," Ted agreed. "I wonder what made it run off that way? It was almost as though someone called it."

"I didn't hear anything, Ted."

"No. But you know there are noiseless dog whistles, pitched too high for people to hear. I wonder if they work with a cat, too?"

"I never heard of their being used for a cat—maybe because a cat won't come unless it feels like it. But if it had been called, Ted, it means this leopard is somebody's pet. I never heard of anyone having a full-grown leopard for a pet, did you?"

"No, and though I suppose a leopard might possibly get accustomed to its trainer, it would still be a threat to other people, and the owner wouldn't dare let it run loose."

"Chances are it just ran off because something scared it off, something maybe too soft for us to hear, or something it could smell and we couldn't."

"But that still doesn't explain what a leopard is doing, running around loose in the woods, and whether anyone is living here. What do you think, Nel?"

Nelson looked around carefully. There were a number of items of home-made furniture about, but no evidences of day-to-day living.

"Someone could have lived here, but I don't think he does now. Maybe the leopard scared him away. Do you notice an animal odor around? That leopard's been in here, no doubt about that. Maybe this is the place where somebody's been keeping it locked up."

"A cabin with windows? That doesn't sound very safe."

"No, but maybe he wasn't worried about safety. Letting a leopard run around loose in the woods isn't very safe, either."

"What I was thinking about," Ted explained, "was that open back door. The leopard may have been going in and out by itself. Nobody may be keeping it here, and maybe it did escape from somewhere."

Nelson looked out through the window. "I can't see any trace of the leopard now, Ted. I think it really took off. What do we do now?

Stay here and wait for somebody to come? Or do we beat it out of here before it gets dark? I know one thing—you won't find me walking through these woods after the sun starts to go down. If a leopard is going to chase me, I want to see it coming a long way off."

"I thought you agreed you couldn't outrun a leopard."

"No, but we could split up, and it would have to decide which one to chase."

"I see," said Ted, half laughing, "you hope it would catch me, and you'd be safe."

"I don't hope for anything of the kind. If I could help you, I'd fight down to the last breath. But if there was nothing I could do, then we'd have to leave it to chance, like tossing a coin."

"Well, I hope things don't get that bad. You have to admit that the leopard hasn't attacked anyone so far, and apparently it has been running loose at least since last Sunday."

"No one as far as we know," Nelson corrected. "We still don't know who lived in this cabin last, or when he left."

To leave or to stay was their immediate problem.

"I wonder what's the best time to go," Ted pondered, "as far as the leopard is concerned? Fortunately, it started off in the opposite direction. I suppose we ought to give it a little time to get a good distance from here."

"Give it too long and it's likely to come back," Nelson argued. "It looks like it's been used to hanging around here. Right now we have a little idea of where it is. If we wait, we won't have any idea."

Between them they decided to wait about ten or fifteen minutes after the cat had left. As they waited Ted looked around. There seemed to be no clue to the cabin's former occupant. What had he been doing for food? The nearest—if not the only—accessible place was the camp at Vanishing Lake. For that matter, what had the leopard been eating? Just that calf?

Nelson had stood impatiently, checking his watch. It was not that he was particularly anxious to get out in the woods where the leopard might stalk them. But it was a danger that had to be faced sometime, and he much preferred action to waiting.

He was ready when the fifteen minutes were up, and cautiously opened the door. With Ted looking over his shoulder, they peered around as well as they could, seeking some sign of the big cat. Nelson looked at the low-hanging limbs around them, and even peeked up at the small canopy above the door, though it was probably too small to support the animal they had seen. A leopard, he had heard and repeated to Ted, liked to attack from the back. If it found that it couldn't attack from the back, it might decide not to attack at all.

But there was no sign of the creature. "All clear here," Nelson announced. "I mean, as clear as we can expect." He stepped outside, and Ted followed, closing the door behind them. They started off down the path leading toward camp, walking side by side as long as they were able, taking fairly long strides, but not rapid enough to invite pursuit.

When the path narrowed, Nelson took the lead, although Ted protested.

"What's the difference?" Nelson returned. "We don't know which is more dangerous, the front spot or the back. We'll just have to take our chances."

They were not a long distance from the lake as the crow flies, but the winding path was not the flight of a crow. Furthermore, though there were still a number of hours of daylight remaining of the long summer day, the shadows were growing longer, and the woods seemed much more dismal and threatening than when they had come. But the real difference was how they felt. Earlier they had merely thought there might be a leopard; now they had definitely seen the animal, or "something." That walk back to the lake seemed much longer than the walk out, though it was mostly downhill, and they were in fact making much better time.

But at last the lake appeared through the trees, and as they got into the boat and shoved away from the shore they sighed with relief. The threat to their lives was over, but the danger to the camp remained.

"What are we going to tell them back at camp?" asked Nelson, who was now at the oars.

"I don't think we ought to tell them anything at all," said Ted, considering carefully. "There's a rule for reporters: find out everything you can and don't tell any more than you have to. A newspaperman does his talking in print."

"But Ted, can we do that? If there really is a serious danger, isn't it our obligation to alert the camp?"

"They ought to be alert by this time. Those two boys have undoubtedly carried their story back to camp."

"But people might not listen to young boys like that," Nelson objected. "They would certainly pay more attention to us. You're a reputable newspaperman."

"Sure, and people know that newspapermen are chiefly interested in a good story. I've got a feeling, Nel, that the people at camp, especially Mr. Armand—and I suppose Mr. Gordon, too—would no more believe our story than they would the story of the two boys."

"But we could do a good job of convincing them, Ted. After all, we *saw* the leopard."

"We saw 'something,' " Ted corrected.

"Well, anyway, we ought to tell them what we saw. Then if they don't believe us, and anything bad happens, at least we won't blame ourselves. What's your objection, Ted?"

"I've got two of them. The first one is that if we tell our story, we're going to become the center of attention, and as long as we're the center of attention, we're going to find it difficult to get to the bottom of this business. At the very least, someone is certain to learn about the baby leopard, and that's something I'd like to keep covered up for the time being. And my second reason is that I don't like anyone using me for his own purposes."

"How do you mean that, Ted?"

"Well, let's look at the matter from the beginning. Mr. Jackson, an elderly man who ordinarily wouldn't be spending his time taking long tramps through the woods, you would suppose, knew exactly where to find those tracks. And he seemed to be awfully well versed on leopards—how did he happen to have all that information? Mr. Armand seemed very reluctant to undertake a hunt for the leopard, and then was very careful to shepherd us away from that critical section of the woods. Was he making a sincere effort to find the leopard, or was there something here he didn't want us to see? Then, too, why was someone so interested in watching us through binoculars? And how did the baby leopard get into your trunk compartment? Did it simply wander in, or did somebody put it there? Then there are Holly and the man who saw the waving grass, although I'd hate to think that *everybody* is in on this thing."

"Ted," said Nelson very seriously, "if someone has a leopard—maybe even a pet leopard that isn't supposed to be very dangerous—and is letting it run loose to scare people, he's playing a very dangerous game."

"I know that, and that's all the more reason for us to move cautiously."

"Well, what are we going to do now, Ted?"

"Keep our eyes and ears open and our mouths shut. And tonight we'll run over to the traveling menagerie and see what we can find out there. One thing we can find out for sure: I want to know if this black cat of ours really is a baby leopard. Judging from my conversation with Doctor Larken, I think it is, but I'd like to have an expert look at it to make sure."

"Why not show it to Doctor Larken, then, instead of Mr. Holland?"

"Because the doctor knows too much about this business already. Mr. Holland may not ask so many questions."

"Well, all right, Ted. I'm with you so far. And as long as we're going over to the menagerie, I'm going to take my camera along. There's no reason why I shouldn't try to get at least a few shots. And one of these days, as soon as we've got a little time, we're going to have to give this whole matter a big, hard think."

When they landed at the pier, they found a number of adults giving them some curious glances, as though guessing their mission, but no one spoke to them more than casually. Ted and Nelson gathered that the younger boys had not been clear about the identity of the two "men" who had gone in pursuit of the leopard. Furthermore, as Ted had anticipated, considerable doubt was cast upon the story told by the boys.

"Fine thing," Nelson growled. "If we were waiting for them to rescue us, we would have had a mighty long wait, I tell you."

"Maybe a lot of people don't like to believe unpleasant things," Ted responded.

"Maybe they don't like hunting for a leopard with their bare hands, the way we did, and maybe they're right. The chances are that they'll live a lot longer than we will."

"Sure, but are they happy?" Ted quoted Nelson's favorite line.

At the cottage they found their cat awaiting them, drooping a little from their long absence but glad to see them. The three had their supper, and got ready to leave for the menagerie. The sky was still bright, and getting the cat to the car in the parking lot without being seen was the problem. Finally they solved it by using a large picnic basket, borrowed from the store where such equipment was rented out. With the cat safely tucked in, they reached the parking lot safely, piled into the car, and headed out of camp.

CHAPTER 14

A GENEROUS OFFER

Holland's traveling menagerie was not a big show, as circuses go. There were bleacher seats set up around the performing arena, but many spectators preferred to stand or walk around. The show was more or less continuous, with animals being brought into the large circle from time to time and put through their paces. Only animal acts were used, and the only human beings who appeared were those who trained and directed the animals, and the girls who rode the elephants and horses.

There were no evening performances, but after a busy day there was an atmosphere of purposeful confusion as Ted and Nelson arrived. Roustabouts ran from here to there, helping to get everything back into shape. The boys learned that Mr. Holland, the owner and manager, also personally trained the big cats. He was pointed out to them, but for some time he seemed so busy that they were hesitant about approaching him.

At last there was a break and they introduced themselves to Mr. Holland. He seemed friendly enough, although still preoccupied with the business at hand.

"You're a newspaper reporter, Ted? Fine, fine. We can always use publicity, and although your paper is a fairly small one, I've heard something of its excellent reputation. Aren't you rather far from home, however?"

"Yes, I am," Ted admitted, "and I'm afraid that I can't promise you any publicity. As you know, town papers like ours usually only use stories with a local tie-in. Actually I'm here for advice."

"Well, advice is easy enough to give. Whether it's worth anything, or whether you decide to take it, is up to you. What is it I can help you with? Oh, Sam! Sam! Don't put Mimi into number two. Number three. O.K."

The boys saw that the big cats were kept in semi-permanent cages where they would have more room and could be seen to better advantage by the public than in their traveling cages. There were some magnificent specimens, many more than they had seen in the zoo at Weatherby, and there was something more electrifying in the atmosphere besides. The boys knew that these animals did more than loll about in their cages. They performed stunts which were difficult for them and represented many months of patient handling by their trainer. And there was an element of danger besides, for who could tell when an animal might suddenly become cantankerous and unmanageable?

"I really have two questions, Mr. Holland, and I'm sure the first one will strike you as very silly. But by any chance has a leopard, or any other animal, escaped from your show?"

"You mean this season? Certainly not. Is that old story going the rounds again? It happens nearly everywhere we go, and we don't try to fight it any more. In the first place there isn't much we can do about it, and in the second place the publicity may be good for the show."

"My second question involves something I want to show you. Have you time to step over to our car? We have an animal there, and we're not quite sure what it is."

"And if you tell us it's just a garden variety of alley cat, we're going to feel pretty foolish," Nelson added.

His curiosity aroused, Mr. Holland followed them to the car. Nelson reached into the car and with a little difficulty grasped the cat and brought it out. For some reason it had turned shy, and clung to him.

"What's this, what's this?" Mr. Holland's manner, at first merely interested, turned into surprise. "Why, it's Wee Willie!"

"Do you know him?" Ted exclaimed.

"Why, I should say I do know him." The animal trainer took the cat from Nelson's arms, and he seemed satisfied to huddle up against him. "I raised him on a bottle. He was given to me by a friend, because his mother refused to nurse him."

"What kind of animal is he?" Nelson inquired.

"Why, this is a black leopard. Can't you tell that?"

The boys exchanged quick glances. "We thought perhaps it was," Ted offered, "but we weren't quite sure. At first we thought that all leopards were spotted."

"Oh, not at all, although those with the most prominent markings command the best prices. But this is a leopard, or you can call it a panther, if you want to. May I ask where you boys found Wee Willie?"

"We were just about to ask where you lost him," said Ted with a laugh.

"Oh, I didn't lose him. As a matter of fact, I sold him. Since I was unable to use him in the show, I had advertised in a trade magazine. If you can't keep an animal, it's best to get rid of it while it's young and may still find a good home—and I suppose the truth is that I don't like to get too attached to an animal I know I can't keep. Monday morning I had a call from the zoo at Weatherby. We agreed to terms, and they sent down a man to pick him up."

"Was Doctor Larken the man you dealt with?"

"No, his name was D. Vollmer. At least that was the name signed on the check. I noticed it was a bank money order, instead of a regular zoo check, but these purchases are often made through private funds instead of going through the official red tape. A baby leopard is a fairly valuable beast, due to the difficulty of raising them in captivity, but of course I was primarily interested in finding a good home for Wee Willie. Now where did you get him?"

"We drove up to the zoo at Weatherby yesterday morning," Nelson explained, "and somehow he must have climbed into my trunk compartment. Anyway, that was where we found him, though not till late last night. I suppose the zoo wasn't as cautious with a little animal like this, the way they would be with a dangerous animal, and maybe they didn't have a proper cage ready for him."

"Well, I suppose you'd better get him back to them as soon as you can. Appealing though he is, he's already almost large enough to badly scratch or maul a small child, and while he would only be defending himself against an annoyance or a threat, the public wouldn't look at it in that light."

"Why is it that you couldn't use him in your show, Mr. Holland?" asked Ted.

"A male leopard is a notoriously difficult animal to train, Ted. Nearly all performing animals are female. I'm not speaking of lions, of course; that majestic mane of the male lion is admired by the public."

"But wouldn't a baby leopard have a particular appeal to children?"

"Yes it would, but this one will only be a baby for a few more weeks. Besides, in a small show like ours, we can't afford to carry animals for exhibition only. They have to perform as well, in order to earn their keep. And of course the fact that this animal is black would be a handicap, unless perhaps I could bill it as a panther, for the American public expects its leopards to be spotted."

"Exactly what is a panther?" asked Nelson, screwing up his face. It seemed that this was a word he had heard misused so often that he no longer was certain what it meant.

"A panther is a leopard. You can stop right there, and you've told the truth. But natives in various parts of the world sometimes use the word *panther* to mean the black leopard, as opposed to the spotted leopard. Of course it makes no kind of scientific sense to have a separate name for animals which may be brothers and sisters and parents to each other, so if the black leopards are panthers, then so are the spotted ones. Our mountain lion is also sometimes known as a panther. Used loosely in this fashion, panther means any large cat."

"I think I understand," said Nelson, nodding his head. "A panther is any animal that you want to call a panther."

"That's about the size of it," Mr. Holland agreed, "and it doesn't matter very much what you decide to call anything, as long as other people know what you mean."

Watching the leopard's affection for his old master, Nelson felt a little tinge of unreasonable jealousy.

"Well, easy come, easy go. I've always heard that cats were treacherous, and that leopards were the most treacherous of all."

"Treacherous?" The word seemed to offend Mr. Holland. "What do you mean by treachery?" Before Nelson could answer, he went on, "I use it to mean that someone has promised you something, either by word or deed, and then proceeded to act in quite a different way. When did a cat ever promise you anything? As a matter of fact, a cat can't be treacherous; it isn't smart enough. It's only people who can be treacherous."

"But isn't it true that an animal which has been friendly before may suddenly turn upon you?"

"No, I don't believe it is true at all, not if you know your animals well, and know the little signs to watch out for. The animals are really talking to you, in their own way. My cats and I understand each other. I don't mean that a cat can fully understand a man, because that's too big a job for any animal, but they understand what I expect of them in the arena. They know that that whip I carry is for showmanship only, and that I will never use it; I don't know of any better way to make an animal savage and unpredictable than to whip it. They do what I want because they know I like and respect them and take good care of them, and why should they break up a mutually advantageous partnership like that? I watch out for them, too. I know the limits of their abilities, and the little things that annoy them, and I don't press them too hard when I see they're out of sorts. When a trainer is set upon by his animals, it is usually for one of three reasons: he was attempting to do more than the animals were ready for; he was stubborn and wanted to show who was the boss; or he was careless.

"I think I could spare a little time," he added, "if you'd like me to show you my big cats."

The boys eagerly jumped at the invitation. The leopard was returned to the car, and Mr. Holland led them past elephants and horses and chimps, a bear, and a seal, to reach the cat menagerie. He liked all animals, but it was apparent that the big cats were his favorites. They passed slowly by the cages, and as they did so Mr. Holland called to each animal. Some seemed to respond slightly, with cat-like dignity, while others remained motionless, and only by the merest flicker of their eyelids betrayed the fact that they were aware of their trainer's presence.

A single leopard was included in the collection, and the boys paused longer here. It was a fine, sleek animal, but was an uncomfortable reminder that a similar animal had been clawing at the roof six feet above their heads only a few hours earlier, apparently intent upon getting in to them. There were several tigers, but the bulk of the collection consisted of lions. The owner stopped in front of one cage, bearing the name Mimi, and it was easy to tell that this was his special favorite of all the animals. Mimi showed it, too, and dragged herself off the floor and over to the bars of the cage, where she strutted and fawned. She was the queen of the show, and knew it.

Nelson remembered his own mission, and requested: "Would it be possible for me to get some pictures of Mimi and some of the others? I don't think the *Town Crier* would be interested in them, but I'm starting to free lance my pictures, and I might be able to sell them."

"I've no objection to that. Any publicity we get would help promote the show, and goodness knows it's difficult enough to keep a show like this one on a profitable basis. But I couldn't let you take any pictures now. The flash bulbs would hurt their eyes, and besides I don't want anything upsetting their routine. You wouldn't get much anyway, sleeping or pacing in their cages. But I'd be glad to help you out tomorrow. We go through a practice run on some of the acts early in the morning, before the public is admitted. You could come right into the arena, and I'm sure you would get some good shots."

Nelson was stunned. "You mean—right into the lions' cage?"

"Why, yes, if you want to. You said you wanted some good shots, didn't you? I'm sure they'd be much better that way than if you tried to take them through the bars, particularly since we have a wire net around the lower part of the bars, where spectators often come quite close."

"Look," Nelson returned, "I know you're trying to be helpful, but this really wasn't what I had in mind at all. Going into the cage is one thing for you—you're used to the animals and they're used to you—but I wouldn't know what to expect. That would make it kind of dangerous, wouldn't it?"

"Not particularly. These are trained cats, you must remember, and I am the person they have been trained to obey. I imagine they would go through their paces in very nearly the same manner as if you weren't there. They're also used to an audience, you know."

"But there is some danger, isn't there?" Nelson persisted, though his voice was a little less forceful now.

"Well, Nelson, I can't guarantee that there is no danger at all, for the unforeseen will occasionally happen. However, don't let me talk you into anything against your wishes. You needn't decide now. Why not sleep on it, and see how you feel about it in the morning?"

They continued on through the enclosure, but Nelson was looking at all these animals in a new light, as possible cage companions on the following day. Their tour here, and through the rest of the grounds, was so interesting that it was with surprise they noted it was ten o'clock—too late to get back to camp.

"Of course we can ring the night bell and someone will let us in, but—" Ted meant that if they did this, the discovery of the baby leopard in their car would be almost certain.

"You needn't leave at all, if you don't care to," Mr. Holland offered. "We have an empty trailer that you're welcome to occupy for the night. There's a telephone available if anyone is expecting you."

"No, no one is expecting us," said Ted slowly. He had no objection to staying, and in fact it seemed the easiest course to follow, but he intended to put no pressure on Nelson to urge him to accept Mr. Holland's invitation. Whatever Nelson decided to do, he would be strictly on his own.

"Fine. I'll have one of the men show you to your wagon, and he can supply you with anything you need."

They were accompanied to the trailer by one of the assistants, who brought them blankets and a few supplies they might have need of. The boys returned to the car for the leopard, and the attendant supplied him with some of the same mess which was fed to the other cats.

The leopard was to remain in the wagon with them all night, and Nelson also took his clock radio to the trailer with them. He had brought it along to camp in case they desired entertainment, news, or a morning alarm clock, but up until now had not taken it out of its carton. In their trailer, which was wired for electricity, he plugged it in, and they listened to the late news. Then they turned out the light, and each crawled into one of the twin beds, the leopard finding a comfortable berth below the foot of Nelson's cot.

"Don't say anything to me, Ted," Nelson ordered. "This is a problem I'm going to have to work out for myself."

"Don't worry, I won't," Ted promised.

"This is going to be a long, hot night for me," Nelson concluded, and turning over noisily, refused to say another word.

CHAPTER 15

A LONG, HOT NIGHT

Ted was awakened sometime during the middle of the night by the leopard cub clawing at his blanket. At first this interruption seemed to blend into a dream, and it took him some moments to realize where he was and what was happening.

"Get down, down," he called quietly, wondering why the animal had leaped up on his bed instead of Nelson's. But deep, sonorous breathing from the other bed suggested to him that the creature had first attempted to arouse his partner, and having failed, came over to try him. In spite of his announced expectation of lying awake all night, Nelson had succumbed.

Then Ted noticed an unnatural glare outside the window, and the unexplained odor of smoke—probably the same thing which was so disturbing the cat—reached his nostrils. He leaped out of bed, and shook Nelson roughly awake.

"Fire! Fire! Let's get out of here fast!"

Nelson was awake and on his feet almost instantly. Ted tried the light switch, but there was no response. The boys threw on their clothes in the dark.

"Anything else we should take?" Ted called, as they prepared to leap out.

"Just the cat and the radio, and I've got the cat."

Ted grabbed for the radio, yanking the plug out of the socket, and they jumped to safety. It was immediately apparent that they were not far from the center of the blaze, which had started only a short distance from their trailer. The trailer itself would go up in a few minutes, and if they had not happened to awaken when they did, the results would have been serious.

"Let's run for the car and get the cat out of the way," was Nelson's order.

"What about a fire alarm?"

"That must have been turned in already. I see some men running around some of the cages. Wonder why they didn't warn us?"

"They probably didn't even know we were here. This trailer was supposed to be empty."

They quickly reached the car, and the two items they had rescued—one animate and one inanimate—were deposited safely inside.

"Wonder if I ought to move the car?" Nelson was speaking almost to himself. "No, it'll be all right here for a while, and there are more important things to be done. Maybe we'll be able to help save some of the animals, but that cat enclosure looks like it's going to be lost, unless the fire department gets here in nothing flat."

Ted was using his breath for running instead of talking, and the boys dashed across the arena to the section where rescue efforts were being organized.

"What can we do to help?" Nelson inquired of the nearest man.

"Can you drive a truck?"

"Yes."

"Then get in, and help pull some of these rolling cages across to that free area. You—" he was pointing to Ted—"give us a hand getting the animals out. Remember that nothing is important except the animals."

Bedlam had descended upon the encampment in just a few minutes. Elephants were trumpeting uneasily, the big cats were all awake and expressing their alarm, the horses were the wildest of all. But the chattering of the chimps and monkeys was most heart-rending, for it was the closest to human sounds in all the wild uproar. The fire was crackling unbelievably, men were shouting everywhere, but all this was as nothing compared to the appeals of the animals. The boys tried to shut it out of their minds, not to hear it, not to understand what it meant.

Suddenly a chimp was thrust into Ted's arms. Whimpering and babylike, it climbed upon his shoulders and clung to him. Ted had no idea what to do with it, until he saw a man with a similar burden run across to a trailer and thrust the animal inside. Ted followed this example, with difficulty extricating himself from the creature's grasp. But there was work to be done, and Ted got rid of the animal to make another trip with another chimp. That seemed to account for all the chimps, and he looked elsewhere.

The elephants had preserved an uneasy dignity, and were being led away. If they had decided to stampede, they might have demolished the camp and put an end to any organized rescue efforts. But somehow they were intelligent enough to know that the best thing was to follow the directions of the humans who were trying to help them.

But the horse-and-pony shed was a contrasting picture of turmoil. The horses had been crazed by the smoke, although they were in no great danger so far. Their rescuers were throwing blankets over their heads and leading them through the haze, keeping tight grips upon their bridles. Though he had had no experience with horses, Ted decided that this was where he was most needed, and took his part with the rest. He led three different horses across the arena to the far side which had not been touched by the fire, and did not seem to be endangered, for the wind was blowing in the opposite direction.

"Tie them good and tight, or they'll run back into the flames," Ted was ordered by one of the men, and he did his best to comply. Apart from the safety of the animals themselves, he realized what havoc they could create in the camp if they were to run about, panic-stricken and unrestrained.

He caught an occasional glimpse of Nelson, still at the wheel of the truck. Everything on wheels, or that could be put on wheels or successfully dragged, was being hauled away to safety. When it came time afterward to count the value of the equipment and animals saved, a good part of the credit would go to Nelson. The other men had picked up his name, and were constantly calling, "Morgan, over here," as he was put from one task to another.

It seemed to Ted, when he dared to take a moment to appraise the situation, that the show would come out of this ordeal in pretty good shape, with one terrible exception. It did not appear now that the cat menagerie could be saved. This had been the first of the main exhibition buildings to catch fire. So far the flames were confined to the front end, and had not reached the animals, who were lined up in cages along the rear wall. But the flames effectively cut off any hope of reaching the animals and transferring them to their traveling cages. It was almost impossible for a man to break in to reach them, and utterly impossible to lead them out to safety.

Ted felt a terrible sympathy for the creatures. He liked the little pet they had found, and these big beasts were simply larger versions with the same basic cat nature. The cats were calling now, not so much in fright as in bewilderment, calling to the human beings they knew to come and help them. The human beings knew that the appeal was futile; did the animals know it, too?

Until now Ted had seen nothing of Mr. Holland, but with his attention centered on the cat menagerie, he saw that the owner and trainer was directing his efforts along this front, hoping somehow to beat back the flames, or at least to open a pathway through them. How pitifully inadequate those narrow streams of water seemed when matched with the mighty flames, and huge, towering billows of smoke. He went up to Mr. Holland, and the trainer ordered him to man one of the hoses, relieving the man who had been holding it for other duties.

Glad to be of some use, no matter how little, Ted took over the hose, and directed it toward the nearest areas where it might do a little good. Once again the futility of their efforts came over him. Unlike the strong fire hoses common to larger communities, the water pressure here was weak, and he could easily manage the hose without assistance. The man he had relieved went off, and Ted suspected that he was trying somehow to scare up added water pressure.

Mr. Holland was here, there, and everywhere, shouting an order to this man, and another to that, meanwhile pitching in wherever his efforts could be a little bit of help.

"If we can only hold the line until the fire department gets here," he rasped out, "maybe we can save them all. We're not licked yet."

Rallied by these words, the men plunged in with renewed hope, and even Ted found his spirits rising a little. The arrival of official help would certainly go far to augment their own efforts, and who knew but what it might be sufficient to turn the tide?

He hated to think about those sleek, handsome, sleepy animals he and Nelson had visited only a few hours before, tried to shut out of his inner vision a picture of what they must be going through now, to drown out their frenzied cries in his ears, by concentrating on the job at hand. The heat from the flames was bringing the sweat to his face, but he retreated not one inch. That little trickle of water he was feeding to the flames seemed to excite them rather than to quench them, but it was all that Ted had to offer.

Had the wind been stronger, the fight would have been lost before it began. But it was only a slight wind, and was not spreading the flames. The things which were feeding the flames were sawdust, hay, burnable temporary buildings, and even a few of the near-by trees which, overhanging some of the buildings, had been ignited by them. Several of these lesser buildings were catching now, but were not causing concern. Ted recognized that they were of little financial value, and that the animals had already been removed from them, but they added spectacularly to the scene, besides contributing more heat, noise, and confusion.

For a time it seemed to Ted they were holding their own, and that while they had not fought back the flames, at least these had not advanced. But once again common sense told him that as long as a fire was burning, it was consuming something, eating up the gains it had already made or advancing imperceptibly. He wondered vaguely how the fire had started, but it was too soon to speculate about that, and too many possible causes were at hand.

But suddenly Ted was sure they were *not* holding their own, that the flames *had* advanced. Almost as soon as a few new hoses were brought up and put into use, the pressure in his own hose, inadequate to begin with, went down. Apparently there was only so much water available, and the more the outlets the less there was for each one. He felt the despair of defeat as the stream he was directing on the fire, now hardly more than a trickle, dissolved immediately into steam and spewed upward.

Then, above all the confusion and flames and shouts and screams of excited animals, he heard the siren of the approaching fire engine. One? No, more than one—he was sure of that, as the first siren seemed to be echoed at a greater distance.

It was only a minute or two longer until the first fire engine roared into the arena, the men dismounting before it had come to a complete stop, only a few feet from the place where Ted was standing. Hoses were swung out in a long line.

"That all the pressure you got?" asked a man, taking the hose from Ted's hands.

"That's all."

"Maybe the bigger hoses will help. If not, we'll have to disconnect some of them. You're not even reaching the main part of the flames with these."

The hoses were shut off, and the thicker hoses strung.

"Can you do anything about that pressure?" Mr. Holland asked the fire chief.

"We'll try. We've got a pump and chemical truck following us."

"Chemicals? Be careful, there're live animals in there."

"You're telling me? I've got ears."

The auxiliary truck was soon there with more fire-fighters, ready to use the pumps, chemicals, and other supplies it had brought. At first Mr. Holland made no protest, as he watched the firemen, but a moment later he was screaming at them, almost incoherently:

"What are you doing?"

"What does it look like we're doing, roasting marshmallows?"

"But you're taking those hoses around the back. You're not even trying to save my cats!"

"Mister, that building is doomed. There's not a thing in the world we could do to save it. But if the woods behind the building catch fire, there's no telling where it will ever stop."

"But you don't understand!" Mr. Holland shouted. "Those are live animals in there, they're mine, they're calling for me to help them."

"Sorry, Mister. I know how you feel. But I can only do what I can do. I hope you've got insurance."

"Insurance! Can insurance policies do tricks? Can I invite the public to come and watch my insurance policies? How much admission should I charge, and do I have to collect an amusement tax?"

"Sorry." The fire chief turned away. Though sorry, he was obviously convinced he could do nothing to save the big cats, and that duty required him to turn elsewhere.

"Listen." Mr. Holland stopped the fire chief before he could get away. "There's just one chance. I can get in there and open the cages. Maybe the cats can get out, and maybe they can't, but at least they'll have a chance to make their dash for freedom."

The fire chief looked at Mr. Holland as though he feared he had lost his mind. "One of us must be crazy, but I don't think it's me.

What happens if those fire-crazed wild animals get loose and start rampaging?"

"They wouldn't. They'd take to the woods."

"And then how would we ever round them up again?"

"They wouldn't be any trouble. They'd quiet down as soon as the panic wore off, and they'd be glad to get back into captivity and safety again."

"I don't know how glad they'd be, and I don't intend ever to find out. Why, if I did that, the townspeople would lynch me, if the judge didn't have me put away. Now look here, Mister. I'm laying down the law to you. Don't you try anything like that, or your show will never appear in this state again, and I'll file charges against you." He called to a couple of his men, "Stand by with your guns. There's a possibility the heat may twist some of the bars, and some of the animals may escape. If they do, shoot them down as soon as they appear. We can't take any chances."

The men nodded and ran off to their stations, and the fire chief departed to direct the fight to save the woods.

A bright light came into Mr. Holland's eyes. He drew a gun from his pocket.

"I'm going in there, Ted. I—" He stopped, as though he wanted to explain, but words were unnecessary, for Ted could read in his face everything there was to be said.

"Good luck, Mr. Holland."

A lion roared, and Mr. Holland called, "Yes, Mimi, I'm coming, I'm coming!"

He dashed off toward the building. The armed guards saw him coming, started to intervene, then shrugged as he dashed into the curtain of flames. Then for the first time Ted turned and ran: ran to find other duties to do, to shut out the sound of shot after shot reverberating above the noisy flames, and the pitiful cries of the big cats being stilled, given the only kind of human help which could reach them, while insatiable tongues of fire lapped at the sky.

CHAPTER 16

THE AFTERMATH

By dawn the fire was out. Firemen scraped at the ashes to uncover any embers which might flare up, while the show people, looking disconsolate and lost, wandered about, searching for anything of value which might still be salvaged. Ted and Nelson, weary from their long night but still too keyed up for sleep, fed their cat, ate a light breakfast themselves, and surveyed the ruins. But somehow they could not bring themselves to approach the site of the destroyed cat menagerie. The events of the night were still too deeply etched in Ted's mind, and Nelson shared his feeling of compassion.

"How brave can you get?" the latter murmured wonderingly. "If Mr. Holland had thought there was a chance of rescuing his cats, I could understand his dashing into the burning building. But he knew that all he could do for them was to save them from a few minutes of terrible suffering. Somehow that seems to make it all the braver."

"He really loved those cats," Ted observed.

"I know. I couldn't have understood it last week, before we found our baby leopard, but I can now."

"I wonder how Mr. Holland is getting along? It was a miracle that he ever got out of that building alive."

"Especially since he didn't seem to care very much whether he got out or not."

They discussed briefly what they ought to do next. Sleep, they felt, was out of the question, and they would wait for that till they got back to camp. They looked around and inquired whether there was anything for them to do, but the circus men, busy trying to re-create order out of chaos, were more competent to handle the necessary duties, and their offer was declined with thanks.

"Well, then, why aren't we on our way home?" Nelson questioned.

"Because we're human beings, and we want to see if there is any way we can help other human beings. I'd like to talk with Mr. Holland before we go."

"What for?"

"Nothing, really—just to let him know how we feel. Of course I'm not going to force myself on him, and if he's too done up to see me, then I'll understand. But I do want to talk with the fire chief, too, and he may want to talk with us. They always inquire around of witnesses, trying to find out how the thing happened."

This was true, and the fire chief carefully noted their names and addresses, before proceeding to other questions. Under his prompting, Ted related exactly how he had been awakened by their cat—he allowed the fire chief to think it was an ordinary domestic cat—and the events that followed.

"I see. I would, of course, like to know exactly where the fire started. Do you have any opinions on that?"

"Well, it seemed to have the best start between our trailer and the cat building."

"Which was it closer to?"

"Our trailer, I suppose, but the wind was carrying it slightly away from us."

"Do either of you boys smoke?"

It was Nelson who spoke up this time, rather sharply. "No, and if we did, we wouldn't have been smoking at that time of night."

"All right, I'm just asking. Now I'd like to see the exact spot where you think the fire started."

The boys showed him, and he examined the place and the area around it.

"Does it really matter how it started?" asked Nelson. "I mean, would the insurance companies refuse to pay off under certain conditions, or anything like that?"

"No, not ordinarily. But of course if there is any possibility that the fire was deliberately started, then it is my duty to inquire into the matter as thoroughly as possible, and turn the evidence over to the police for following up."

"Do you have any reason to suspect arson?" asked Ted, frowning.

"No, not particularly, and of course in a show like this one I can see many ways in which a fire could be started through ordinary carelessness. But I may as well tell you that Mr. Holland himself seems to suspect arson."

"He does! But why?"

"Oh, he has built up a chain of evidence in his own mind. I admit I had difficulty following him—he wasn't quite coherent when I talked with him, so I felt I'd better put it off. But ordinarily the principal reason for arson is to collect insurance money. I've made a few discreet inquiries, and apparently it is no secret that the show was short of money, that it might have had difficulty getting through the season. Of course if insurance money was the object, then it must have been Mr. Holland himself."

Ted shook his head. "Not Mr. Holland. You would never believe that, if you knew how he loved those big cats."

"Well, I'm not seriously concerned over the possibility, but I'll have to look into it, particularly if Mr. Holland continues to press me for an investigation."

"A guilty man wouldn't try to stir up an investigation, would he?" asked Nelson, incredulous.

"Sometimes they do it to divert suspicion from themselves. Sometimes they do it because they have a guilty conscience, and actually want to get caught. By the way, Ted, you were present when I was arguing with Mr. Holland last night. You know there was nothing else I could have done, don't you?"

"Yes," Ted agreed, "as long as you think people are more important than animals."

"That's what I'm paid to think, I suppose."

"And you wanted to save the woods, and you did," Nelson pointed out.

"I'm not going to say I don't feel bad about the way things turned out, but the only possible thing I could have done was to order a battalion of men into that building. That was something I couldn't have done under these circumstances, maybe not even if there had been people inside instead of animals. You see, I've been through things like this before—fires in which it *was* people instead of animals, and I had to decide whether or not to try to rescue them. Sometimes I've had to say no—the risk was too great. Maybe I've been wrong sometimes."

He turned away sadly and they could tell that for all the hardening effect of his past experiences, he still felt the tragedy of situations like this.

They walked over to Mr. Holland's trailer to inquire about him. They gave their names to the attendant in charge, saying they wanted to say good-by. He spoke with Mr. Holland, and then invited them in. Knowing the doctor had been there, they expected to find him in bed, but he was sitting in a big easy chair, still shaken from his ordeal, bandaged here and there though he seemed to be all right physically. But his spirit seemed to have been crushed.

"I've spoken with some of my men, and from what they tell me, I have a good deal to thank you both for. We here were just doing our duty, and I suppose the firemen were, too. But when strangers pitch in to help, it seems to mean a little more."

"We had to do the little we could," Nelson replied.

Ted shook his head sadly. "But it wasn't enough."

"We hope you'll soon be feeling better, sir," Nelson offered, "and that you'll soon have the show back on the road again."

"Thank you, Nelson, but the show is finished. The insurance won't cover the loss, and if we miss this season's attendance—Besides, what could I do without my big, lovely cats—Helene, with her little way of twitching the tassel on her tail when she was annoyed, Susie and her love of hamburgers, and my little prima donna, Mimi—" Here his voice choked, and he was unable to go on.

The boys felt embarrassed, and tried to change the subject. "You don't really believe the fire was the work of any arsonist, do you?" Ted questioned.

"Yes, I do, Ted. You helped give me the idea."

"I did?" he asked in surprise.

"Yes, with your story of the escaped leopard. It's the kind of story people always spread when they want to hurt a show. But that's not all. I know some of the people in the area don't like us. Whether they are afraid of escaped animals or what I don't know, but they've tried to get our lease canceled. I don't mind when people deal with you on an open basis, but a good many of them don't stop there. Last year one of our lions was poisoned. Boys think it smart to toss firecrackers into the cages. I could go on, but what's the use? I don't think I'll ever again give anyone a chance to hurt the animals I love. You see, when you put animals in a cage, you take away their ability to take care of themselves, and so it becomes your obligation to take care of them. Sometimes you don't do a very good job, just as I failed last night. I couldn't protect them from some person's villainous meanness."

"You speak about mean people," Nelson pointed out, "but there are the other kind, too. And I'm sure many people, especially children, learn to love and respect animals just from watching a show like yours."

"Maybe they do, Nelson, maybe they do. But from now on they'll have to learn somewhere else. This show is finished. And do you know why it is finished? Because people are afraid. If I could have let my animals out, some of them could have been saved. But I couldn't do it because people would have been afraid of them."

"But someone might have been hurt by them," Ted observed.

"Yes, I know, they might have been hurt because they wouldn't have known how to deal with a frightened animal, an animal that had been frightened by something that people did in the first place. It is people who cause the trouble, and the animals who have to suffer for it."

Ted explained quietly, "But you know, Mr. Holland, we really did see some animal up in the woods—we think it's a leopard. We ran into a cabin, and it sprang up on the roof and clawed awhile, before running off."

Mr. Holland showed a flicker of interest. "A big cat, you say. You know, things are pretty settled around here, but a mountain lion might possibly have drifted in somehow."

"With spots?" asked Nelson.

"Well, no, it doesn't have the well-defined spots of the leopard. Still, it would be interesting to track some of these rumors down and see just what is back of them. The truth is, I have to get away from the show this afternoon. Certain things are going to happen that I just couldn't stand. Maybe a little excursion like this would help me get my mind off things here. And while we're about it, we could run Wee Willie back up to the zoo in Weatherby. Leave him here for now, if you like. You go home and get some rest, and I'll drive over early this afternoon."

"They have some lion cubs up at the zoo," Ted offered. "Maybe you could make a deal for them."

"No, no, I wouldn't be interested in that. But I would like to see them," he admitted.

The boys took their leave, putting the baby leopard in charge of one of the attendants. They drove slowly back toward the camp.

"Stop at a phone booth, will you?" Ted requested. "What for?"

"Thursday morning. My deadline is noon. We've just been through an unusual night, to say the least."

"You sure Mr. Dobson will want the story? There's no local angle."

"Well, that's up to him to decide. At least I want to let him know I'm earning my salary. Another thing, I want to call the health department, and see if they have that report on the water yet. I might as well clear up all the loose ends I can."

The calls were made, and Ted returned to the car.

"Well, what next, Ted? Wouldn't it be nice if we could spend just a couple of days swimming, fishing, and playing tennis? But I suppose we can't do it. We've got too many things to figure out. Just to think that yesterday afternoon we were afraid of a little old leopard on the roof! Now I don't think it would scare me so much. Leopards are just big cats, and they've got their problems, too. I wouldn't care to get cozy with them, but all I ask is that they let me alone and I'll let them alone."

"Just now," said Ted, yawning, "I feel too tired to be afraid of anything. Did I tell you the water checked out all right? No typhoid. Let me off at the office building and I'll tell Mr. Armand, in case he didn't get the report yet."

"Heck with Mr. Armand."

"But Mr. Gordon's been kind to us."

When Ted went into the office, he found Mr. Armand presiding at the desk.

"Did you get the report on the water test?" asked Ted.

"No, not yet. I've had a thousand and one things on my mind. Besides, I called them yesterday afternoon, and they promised they would call *me* when the test was ready, so I figured it wasn't finished yet."

"There must have been a slip up. I spoke to them a few minutes ago, and they said the water tested out all right. I thought you'd like to know, for Mr. Gordon suggested putting up posters guaranteeing the purity of the water, to relieve people's minds."

"Of course I'm glad to hear it," said Mr. Armand shortly, though he certainly looked more annoyed than pleased. "But I wish people would call me when they promise, and I wish Mr. Gordon wouldn't find twice as many things for me to do as I have time for. And although I'm obliged to you for clearing up the matter for me, I surely would have called the health department in a little while anyway."

As Ted thought about it, he could hardly blame Mr. Armand for being a little annoyed. Doubtless, he figured that Ted would carry this story to Mr. Gordon, and the camp owner might feel that the manager had been neglecting his duties.

"Well, I thought you'd like to know," said Ted cheerfully. He started to leave, then turned back, thinking this might be a chance to check up on Mr. Jackson's story. "Do you remember that man who spoke to you in the woods just as we were starting out on the leopard hunt?"

"No, I don't. Oh, yes, come to think of it I do. What about him?"

"Do you know who he is?"

"I think his name's Kyhoe, or something like that. He has the farm that adjoins the woods."

"Would you mind telling me what he said to you?"

"I don't know why you should be interested in him, but I don't mind telling you. He claimed that one of his animals had been slain. Well, maybe it's true, maybe it isn't. But I didn't see that that had anything to do with a leopard in the woods. More likely there's a sheep-killing dog loose in the neighborhood."

Mr. Jackson had said it was a calf that was killed, but Ted decided not to press the point.

"I assured him that there was no leopard in the woods, and that we were just going through the motions to satisfy some of the guests. Then he left, and that's the last I saw of him."

"Thank you."

"Oh, Ted—" Mr. Armand called to him as he started to leave once more. "This is Thursday, and that's your deadline morning, isn't it?"

"Yes."

"Did you phone in a story? You know that I'm anxious the camp shouldn't get any unfavorable publicity."

"I spoke to my editor a little while ago, but he won't be using anything about the leopard in the woods. It's just a rumor so far."

"All right, Ted, thank you. I'm glad you were able to help me out."

It was on the tip of Ted's tongue to tell him that he hadn't done it for him, but he decided there was no use and took his departure.

"Now me for that lake, Ted," said Nelson, when Ted rejoined him. "We've been here since Monday, and haven't been in it yet. Haven't we got time for a dip?"

"We'll take time."

On the way down to the beach, they met the twins' mother, and Ted inquired about Jeff.

"Oh, he's coming along all right. It was just a little attack of tonsillitis. I suppose we were silly to get so excited about it, but he was restless and complaining and there seemed to be a little hitch in his breathing, so we thought it best not to take chances. We're bringing him home tonight."

"Then there wasn't any question of typhoid?"

"Oh, certainly not. Those typhoid stories must have started in connection with something else."

Then they finally had a swim and returned to their cottage for a few hours of sound sleep.

CHAPTER 17

LOLA

As he had promised, Mr. Holland came over soon after lunch and they started off in two cars.

At the Weatherby zoo, they entered Dr. Larken's office, and he was shown the animal.

"Oh, so *that's* the leopard you were speaking of over the phone, Wilford. A fine little animal, but this certainly rates as a big surprise. I don't know where you managed to find him."

"He's yours, isn't he?" asked Ted, with narrowing eyes. The question of why the doctor had failed to mention the baby leopard over the telephone had long been on Ted's mind.

"Certainly not. Don't you suppose I'm acquainted with all our larger animals? Not that I wouldn't like to have him, though."

"But I sold him to this zoo just last Monday," Mr. Holland objected.

"You did? That's news to me. With which person did you deal?"

"A man named D. Vollmer."

Dr. Larken shook his head. "There's no one by that name associated with this zoo."

Ted looked puzzled. "But if you didn't buy him, then who is D. Vollmer, and what did he want with a baby leopard?"

"Publicity, obviously," put in Mr. Holland. "You are gentlemen of the press, and somebody is trying to get you interested in this story, for some reason or other. I suppose they didn't expect you to come to me with the baby."

"Are you sure *you* aren't the guilty party?" asked Dr. Larken with a laugh. "Publicity is all part of show business, isn't it?"

"I'm afraid I must plead not guilty. The show would have been gone by the time Ted's story came out. And even if I did want that kind of publicity, it wouldn't do me any good now."

"I know," said the doctor sympathetically. "I heard about your fire. Well, come on. I want to show you our lion cubs."

He led the group to the cage from which the screen had now been removed. "They're just about big enough to leave their mother," he explained, "and when I take them away I'm going to run into a space problem. Are you sure I couldn't interest you in a trade? Three lion cubs for the leopard cub."

"No, I guess I wouldn't have any use for them now," said Mr. Holland slowly. But he lingered at the cage a little longer than the others, and turned back to look at them again as they left.

Dr. Larken agreed to look after the baby leopard until its ownership could be determined. He then asked them about the reputed leopard in the woods, and Ted filled him in with everything that had happened. The zoo keeper turned to the animal trainer.

"A cat about the size of a leopard, with spots and a long tail, but apparently tame, or at least partly trained. Don't you think it's a—"

"Sh, don't spoil the boys' fun," Mr. Holland cautioned. True to the traditions of the show, he didn't care to reveal his star turn too early.

"Well, I surely wish I could go along with you to find—it," said Dr. Larken regretfully, "but I'm due at a budget hearing today. As usual they don't want to give me as much money as I think I need, and I'll have to explain to them again how much one of these big animals eats in a day."

Back at their cars, they held a brief discussion as to the best way to reach the cabin in the woods again. Of course the closest way was through the camp at Vanishing Lake, but Ted was set against it.

"I've got a feeling that there's someone at camp watching everything we do, and that whoever is out in the woods will be tipped off that we're coming."

This posed a problem, for the only other approach by road was the highway beyond the deep woods, and this meant a long walk for them. But Mr. Holland said it was all right with him, and this route was decided upon. They reached the spot after half an hour's drive, parked their cars, and got out.

"There's just one thing I'd like to know before we start out," said Nelson sternly. "Are we in any danger, or are we not? I mean, if it isn't a leopard, it's at least nice to know what's going to eat you up."

"If my guess is correct, we're not in any danger."

It turned out that the highway was indeed farther away than Mr. Armand had indicated the afternoon of the leopard hunt. But at last they approached the cabin, after a walk of nearly two hours. There was no sign of life about. The front door was tightly closed, and when they walked around the back, they found that door closed, too. They looked through the windows, but these were too dirty to show what was inside.

"Well, let's go in," Mr. Holland invited them, and threw open the door. As he did a great cat leaped through the air at the animal trainer.

"Get down, get down," he ordered, fending it off. Then he exclaimed in surprise, "Why, it's Lola! Come here, Lola. How've you been? She likes this," and he proceeded to scratch her behind the ear.

Only slightly reassured, the boys followed him into the darkened cabin.

"You mean you know her?" Nelson demanded.

"Oh, yes, Lola and I were good friends, years ago. She did a number of turns for me."

"Then if you know her, you must know her owner," Ted pointed out.

"No, not any more. I knew she had been sold, after leaving me, and the chances are she's changed owners a number of times."

In spite of the ease and calmness with which he treated the animal, Ted and Nelson remained wary.

"Oh, come on," Mr. Holland encouraged them. "Lola is perfectly harmless. In fact, I'm sure you've made her acquaintance already."

"Yes," Nelson recollected, "and she was sniffing at the roof as though she was terribly anxious to get at us."

"Wouldn't you have done the same thing if you knew that strangers were in your home? You know how many dogs will bark and bark when a visitor arrives. They don't mean harm. They just want to let the visitor know that this is *their* home."

The boys advanced, but somewhat gingerly. They could see now that the animal wasn't *quite* a leopard. It was about the same size as a leopard, but the shade of color was a little different, and the spots were individual, instead of in groups, or rosettes. Lola lifted her head with interest as they approached, but remembering the fright she had given them before, the boys were still reserved.

"What kind of animal is it?" asked Ted.

"It's a cheetah, of course, sometimes known as the 'hunting leopard,' though actually it isn't a leopard at all."

"But the resemblance is so strong. Surely they must be closely related."

"Not as closely as you might think. The same family grouping, but not the same genus. Scientists always want to classify animals according to their bones and tissues, and then a cheetah is properly a cat. I sometimes wonder why they don't classify instead according to intelligence, habits, and temperament? In that event a cheetah might find itself in the dog family instead."

The boys remained a little doubtful. The cheetah looked so much like a cat that they were unwilling to accept her on any other basis. Mr. Holland sought to prove his point. He lifted one of Lola's paws, and showed them the underside.

"You see that the claws do not retract fully, as with the cat. You know that a hunting animal must depend either on speed or on stealth to catch its prey. A cat generally relies on stealth, whereas a dog relies on speed; the cat's best weapon is its claws, and a dog its teeth. A pursuing animal must have *greater* speed than its prey, otherwise the prey could escape by means of its headstart and by dodging tactics. The cheetah is built for speed, being the fastest four-footed animal on earth. It can reach a speed of seventy miles an hour."

"When the wind gets that fast, they call it a hurricane," Nelson remarked.

"Contrast that with a horse's speed of about forty-three miles per hour, and a man's four-minute mile. A cheetah has a flexible backbone, which gives it an advantage over the horse. And slow-motion studies of its pace show that a cheetah is off the ground twice in each complete stride—when its four legs are extended inward, and when they are extended outward—while a galloping horse is only completely off the ground when its four legs are inward. Have I convinced you now?"

"You've convinced us that a cheetah is fast." Ted laughed. "I don't think you've convinced us it's quite the same as a dog."

"Oh, but temperamentally it is, Ted. It is one of the few animals that is customarily captured as an adult—after it has taught itself to hunt—and then tamed. Most animals would be untamable after they had grown up wild. Even the ordinary house cat, if it was raised wild, wouldn't make a very suitable pet."

Ted sat down on a bench, but before Nelson could sit down beside him, Lola had taken the vacant spot. She nestled herself very close to him, and began to lick his ear.

"Do you have hair tonic on?" Ted nodded, wishing that he did not. "Lola is very fond of hair tonic. If she gets to annoying you, give her a shove."

It did not seem to occur to the man that Ted might not like Lola's attentions, or would hesitate to push the beast away. Having given Ted's left ear a thorough washing, Lola began to work along the fringe of his hair, around the back of his neck. That rough tongue felt rather strange, but Ted would certainly have hesitated about shoving away a much stronger animal that weighed almost as much as he did. Besides, Lola's resemblance to the leopard was so strong that Ted could hardly trust her allegedly gentle nature.

"Somebody must have been taking care of Lola," Ted remarked when Lola finally settled down. "Do you suppose it's her owner?"

"Maybe not, Ted. There are theatrical agencies which rent out animals for performing or for stunts of this kind. For obvious reasons the nature of the deal is often kept private, although I suppose the renter usually has to show some indication of good character, and that he is capable of handling the animal. With dangerous animals, the restrictions would be greater, but a trained cheetah, you see, would be considered relatively harmless."

"But if we sat here long enough, we'd find out who's coming here to take care of her, wouldn't we?"

"I doubt it. I don't think he will show up until after we are gone."

"Just the same, there can't be very many agencies where a cheetah can be rented. Couldn't we check with them and find out who it is?"

"I imagine you'd run up against a dead end. I think I know the name of the man. It is probably D. Vollmer again. Evidently he bought the leopard cub to place in your car for the purpose of securing publicity, and building up the idea of a mother leopard out in the woods. There were also to be a few glimpses of the 'leopard' in the woods, and after the reputation of the animal was well established,

Lola would be whisked out of sight and returned to the agency. That was the part you newspapermen were expected to play."

"But we *didn't* play," Nelson pointed out. "We were careful not to give the leopard any publicity."

"And probably that's the very reason this thing has been carried on so long."

"But what sort of publicity was he after—good or bad?" Ted questioned.

"I could see where some misguided person might believe that a tale of a leopard in the woods would attract business to the resort. But tell me first—have there been any other rather startling things happening around camp?" Ted told about the brush fire and the typhoid scare, and the man nodded. "Then it was bad publicity that was wanted. Someone seems to have a grudge against the camp or some of the personnel there. Or it might be the work of a rival resort. I'll leave that up to you. I'm just thankful that I've run down one of these rumors at last. Lola wants you to scratch her back of the ear, Ted."

Ted looked very thoughtful as he complied.

CHAPTER 18

A GOOD, HARD THINK

After Mr. Holland had driven off, Ted and Nelson stood for a few minutes leaning against their car, talking things over.

"Does this end the story for us, Ted? Of course I'd like to see how everything comes out, but does it really concern us?"

"Somebody has been trying to use us for his own purposes, and I don't like it. That concerns us, doesn't it?"

"Yes, and when I think of what almost happened to little Jimmy in the brush fire, I want to see it through to the end. What we must do is give this thing a good, hard think. Who do you think put that baby leopard in the car?"

"That would depend on *when* he was put in. I don't believe now that it happened on our trip to Weatherby, and I don't think it happened at the drugstore."

"What about in the parking lot?"

"It was still light when we left for the drugstore. It would have been tricky to manage with so many people still around. No, I think the best guess is that it happened in the woods across the lake, and I hope someone was watching us later to make sure we found him so he wouldn't starve. After all, what can a newspaper reporter do when he discovers a baby leopard in his car? He surely will do something with him, and chances are he'll write a story about him, too. Why not? It's his story, and if he doesn't, one of his rivals may get hold of it. Now who do we *know* was over in the woods that afternoon?"

"Mr. Armand or one of his men?"

"I don't see how any of them could have done it. Remember we were all in a line, and no one could have been missing from the line without someone else knowing it, unless *all* the men were in on it. Besides, they all showed up when we assembled at the other end of the woods. Who else?"

"You mean the farmer, Mr. Kyloe?"

"That's just the man I was thinking of. Look at it this way, Nel. Somebody's been taking care of the cheetah. Could it be somebody from camp? That doesn't seem likely because how would he manage to get over here so often without arousing suspicion?"

"What about the man who swam across the lake during the night?"

"Yes, it's possible that he swam across because of something connected with the cheetah. But I think there would have to be two of them in it together. I imagine that man on the bridge who was watching us the first time had some sort of signal arranged to tell someone else over in the woods that we were coming. The cheetah was supposed to be released so we'd catch a glimpse of her. Then we'd come back and spread the story around, and you would be useful with your camera."

"But the man wasn't on the bridge the next time we went across," Nelson objected.

"No, but I'll bet he was still watching us, from some other spot that had been arranged. The signal was passed when we approached the other shore, but as it happened those two boys saw the cheetah first."

"Then I suppose our next move, Ted, is to visit the Kyloe farm and see if we can pick up anything."

Ted considered. "Yes, I suppose that's about all there is to do. But I'm not very much interested in Mr. Kyloe. Suppose he is the person who has been taking care of the cheetah. We don't know how guilty he really is. He may have been led to believe that this was just a harmless publicity stunt. The man I'm really interested in is the one in camp who's directing things."

"At least we know it isn't Mr. Jackson. He couldn't swim across the lake."

"That's for sure. I imagine Mr. Jackson is just what he seems to be—a gossiping old man. But I'll bet someone has been using him, just the way we've been used. In one way or another, he's been fed little items of gossip which he passes around. He's been on this leopard story from the beginning, and whoever called the health department for a check on the water must have handed him a line about possible typhoid."

"But those tracks, Ted—how do you suppose such an old man ever found them in the woods?"

"They probably had tracks all over the place, so that he'd have had trouble missing them."

The drive to the Kyloe farm was a short one, and they turned up the drive. A man came out from the barn to meet them.

"Are you Mr. Kyloe?" asked Ted.

"No, I'm just the hired man around here. But maybe I can help you."

"I'm a newspaper reporter. I hear you had a calf killed by a leopard."

The man grinned. "*I* never said it was a leopard. A savage dog would seem more likely to me." He added mysteriously, "But I could think of something even more likely than that."

"What?"

"Something on two legs," he said in a whisper.

"You mean a person?"

"Well, why not?" He raised his voice only slightly. "The fact is, I noticed some footprints outside the fence that weren't mine, and I don't *think* they were there the night before that. Well, come on. I was told if anyone came around asking, I was supposed to show them the place."

He led them to the corner of a pasture near the woods. No traces of the deed remained, except that the grass had been trampled around the scene. The boys were more interested in the fence. It seemed substantial enough. Of course a big, active animal like a leopard could have leaped over it—except Lola wasn't a leopard, and Mr. Holland had assured them that Lola was gentle. A human culprit now seemed the more likely bet, as the hired man had suggested.

"Does Mr. Kyloe own this farm?" Ted asked.

"No, I believe he just rents it. The real owner is a man named Vollmer. But I have never seen him. I guess he doesn't give a darn about the farm, as long as he collects his rent money."

Mr. Vollmer again! The boys were convinced that they were chasing a phantom, for they no longer believed a man by that name existed. He was an alias for someone back at camp—but who?

They thanked the man, and drove slowly back toward camp.

"If we could only find out who D. Vollmer is," Nelson emphasized, "but I don't suppose we can. He's probably covered his tracks pretty well. Probably Mr. Kyloe knows who it is, but he won't tell."

"Wait a minute." Ted was thinking hard. "There just might be a way to find out. What's the county seat around here?"

"Dalton. Why?"

"Can we drive over there now, before the courthouse closes?"

"Do you know it's after six o'clock? But we can stop there if you want to. It's not much out of our way."

They did stop, and found that while the courthouse was officially closed, an obliging clerk was willing to let them consult the deeds. Ted had explained along the way what they were looking for, but Nelson remained skeptical. However, the clerk found the correct deed, and showed it to them. These were, after all, public records for people to consult when they wanted to check the ownership of property.

Ted looked the document over carefully. The name of the owner of the Kyloe farm was given as Hans Armand.

The boys thanked the clerk, and went out to the car, where they sat in stunned silence for some moments. It was Mr. Armand, then, who was the mysterious Mr. Vollmer.

At last Nelson asked, "But why did he buy the farm in his own name, Ted?"

"Because buying property under a phony name is a pretty tricky business, if you want your title to be good. Anyway, he bought the farm two years ago. Maybe his intentions *were* good at that time. It was only afterward that he began to get different ideas."

"Then you think Mr. Armand was back of the whole thing? But what was his purpose? You'd think that anything that hurt the camp would hurt him, as long as he was managing it."

"I suppose it would, if he was planning on remaining a manager all his life. But suppose he had designs on becoming the owner? If he could force Mr. Gordon to sell at a low price, then he could take over. The leopard scare was one of the devices he used, and that was where we came into the picture."

"But it was Mr. Jackson who decided to call the *Town Crier*."

"I know, but I'll bet that Mr. Armand somehow put a bug in his ear. Maybe Mr. Jackson asked for the name of a reputable paper around here, and Mr. Armand mentioned our paper."

Nelson laughed. "With all due respect to present company, Ted, I don't think Mr. Armand decided upon the *Town Crier* because of its reputation. I'll bet he wanted to interest a paper that wasn't *too* close, with a reporter who might not nose .around here *too* much. We were supposed to pick up this leopard yarn, then go home, and that would end it. But you did just what he didn't want you to do by finding his name on that deed."

"Oh, Mr. Armand undoubtedly had a lot of angles," Ted agreed. "I remember the first time we talked with him he suggested someone might be trying to wreck the camp. Of course that was to turn suspicion away from himself. And I imagine he knew just how to handle Mr. Jackson. By seeming to oppose the old man constantly, he got his dander up, and in this way made him do exactly what he wanted him to."

"What about that argument he had with Mr. Kyloe in the woods? Were we supposed to hear that?"

"Oh, I imagine we were. And we thought Mr. Armand was leading us astray in the woods so we wouldn't discover anything. Now I think it was just the opposite. He was trying to arouse our curiosity so that we *would* go back. And if we went we were almost certain to discover the cabin. There's only the one main path, plus the one branch off that would have taken us back into the old section and so we would probably disregard it. Mr. Kyloe must have put the cub in our car, after Mr. Armand piled all the men into his car so we had to take ours along."

"Do you think he swam across the lake that night just to butcher that poor little calf?"

"I suppose he did, or at least to help, if Mr. Kyloe was in on that part of it, too. His car might have been heard, and he couldn't take a boat without the boat-tender knowing it. I don't think the hired man knew anything about this; he was too straightforward with us. He was just another of their dupes."

Nelson hesitated. "I believe all this, Ted. It's the only way to explain things so they make sense. But now that we know it, what are we going to do about it? Do we really have enough proof to do anything at all?"

"We know that Mr. Vollmer purchased the black leopard. We think that he rented the cheetah. We know that he was the owner of the farm, and that it is registered under Mr. Armand's name. That ought to be enough evidence to lay before Mr. Gordon. He'll know what to do next."

Upon returning to camp, Ted asked for an interview with Mr. Gordon, and the owner came over to their cottage.

"I have just one question, Mr. Gordon. Have you received an offer to buy this camp, and was one of the purchasers named D. Vollmer?"

"Why, yes, Ted, he was."

"Did you ever see Mr. Vollmer?"

"No. The offer was made through an attorney."

Then Ted proceeded to tell him all the evidence they had uncovered. As he talked, Mr. Gordon's face grew more and more thoughtful.

"You've presented a pretty good case, Ted, and I think I can add to it. From what you've told me of that farm, I don't believe Mr. Armand is making any serious effort to work it. He intended it for another purpose entirely: an extension of the camp here. At first perhaps he merely hoped to sell the farm to me for a good price; then he thought of running it as a rival to our camp here; and finally he planned to get control of this camp and run them together. He always has had big ideas, and I imagine he thinks he could run the camp more efficiently than I am doing. For that matter, I could run it more efficiently, too, if I could buy it at a near-bankruptcy price, as he no doubt hoped to do. I didn't know, of course, that he had bought the farm, but he must have realized afterward that he couldn't run it as a separate resort because it doesn't have sufficient frontage on the lake. With both, it might work out, although there are reasons why I am not interested in expanding at this time. Mr. Armand is acquainted with my financial arrangements here, and he knows that I am operating to a large extent on borrowed money. If I can't renew my loans this year, I'm in trouble. And if he could make sure the camp had a poor year, he could be pretty sure I wouldn't be successful with my loans."

"What are you going to do about it, Mr. Gordon?" asked Nelson.

"I suppose I could simply dismiss Mr. Armand and let it go at that. The leopard story and the typhoid scare can be overlooked, I suppose, since they did no lasting damage. But that brush fire and little Jimmy are a different matter. Even if he didn't know the boy was in the shed, he must be held responsible for what happened as a result of the fire he started. And there's no telling what else he had planned for the future.

"I'm very grateful to you boys for what you've done, for I never believed there was a leopard in the woods, and would never have done anything about it. Without your efforts, Mr. Armand might have had his way. But I'll carry the ball from here on. If I should need your testimony I'll let you know, but I don't think I will. If this lawyer is a reputable man, he's going to object to being used as a front for a scheme like this, and I think I'll be able to get the evidence I need."

CHAPTER 19

A LOOSE END

The time came to say good-by to Gerald and Holly, and Gerald especially seemed sorry that he was going to lose two willing tennis players. He suffered from the problem of the good player who is unable to find good enough players to oppose him, but their doubles sets had been fun.

"I hope we can get together for some more tennis sometime," he said, shaking hands. "Perhaps we shall."

"I'm sure of it," said Holly warmly. "It's a small world."

"Sure it is," Nelson agreed. "You can cross the whole country in a few hours by jet."

"But look at all you've missed," said Ted with a laugh, and the group broke up.

There had been no showdown between Mr. Gordon and Mr. Armand so far, since the owner was anxious to consult the attorney first. But the boys were glad to find a substitute clerk at the desk when they turned in their keys. They didn't want to see Mr. Armand again.

In the back seat of the car was their clock radio which they had never used except that one night. They moved it in order to make room for some of their stuff. Ted did this without thinking of anything special, but some mental process must have been started, for when Nelson was about to turn left into the main road, Ted ordered him to take the opposite turn.

"What for?" asked Nelson, perplexed.

"We're going back to the menagerie. There's still a loose end we can clear up."

At the menagerie, they located the manager.

"Mr. Holland, what time was the fire alarm turned in?" Ted asked immediately

"At two twenty-six."

"Yes, that was about what I thought, but it was so hard to estimate or keep track of time in all that confusion. But, Mr. Holland, we had a clock radio plugged in at our trailer, and the electricity went off at one twenty-five. Don't you see what that means?" he asked, as the others looked at him questioningly. "Our electricity went off an hour before the fire was reported. You remember that our trailer was a little set off, and there was a long electric wire leading to it. I remember now that the wire ran close to a tree, and I'll bet that a branch rubbing against it rubbed it through until it broke. The live wire may have landed on a pile of sawdust, or some dry leaves, or an oil slick, ignited it, and in the hour that passed before the fire was discovered it had grown too big to control. By the time we went over the spot later with the fire chief, it was too late to prove anything. I'm sure you'll remember the wire and the tree. Can't you?"

Mr. Holland looked at the others thoughtfully. "Then the fire here really didn't have anything to do with the trouble up at Vanishing Lake?"

"Not a thing," Ted assured him.

"That *does* sort of put a new slant on things. I couldn't bring myself to expose my cats to wanton viciousness, but an accident is part of the risk of living."

"Sure, it is," said Nelson stoutly.

"And you could still take Doctor Larken up on his offer of the three lion cubs," Ted urged him.

"Hm-m. It isn't that it would be difficult for me to get lion cubs, but this would mean I could get started right away. Except for the big cats, we've still got a pretty good show left, and I'll bet I could have some of these acts together before the season's over."

He grew increasingly excited. "But of course I'll have to discuss it with some of my assistants." He excused himself and hurried off, but the boys already knew what the final decision would be.

Nelson decided he wanted to do a little tinkering with the car, and Ted looked in on the chimps he had helped to rescue. By the time he returned, he found Mr. Holland talking to Nelson. The happy smiles on both faces were all the proof Ted needed that the show was going to go on.

"Come and see us next year," Mr. Holland invited them in parting, and the boys promised to try.

"Well, I didn't get my pictures, but did you get a story? Or is this a wasted trip as far as the newspaper is concerned?" Nelson asked as he turned off the gravel road and on to the highway.

"Oh, I got my story." Ted laughed. "Mr. Dobson told me it's in print already, and we'll be reading it when we get back to Forestdale. Don't you know what it is? You ought to, because you were in it. 'LOCAL BOYS HELP RESCUE MENAGERIE ANIMALS IN FIRE.' There's a story for you, even if it didn't happen near Forestdale."

"Well, pardon my blushes! Can you really write a story like that about yourself?"

"Why not? There won't be any name on it, so the readers won't know who wrote it. Of course Mr. Dobson actually put it down on paper, and I didn't tell him anything except the truth."

"Anyway, the truth the way you saw it. That doggoned little black leopard, though! I'm going to miss him, won't you, Ted?"

"Yes, I guess so. You know, it's possible that he saved our lives, waking us up that way."

"Maybe we wouldn't have been there if it hadn't been for him."

"I don't know about that. We might have gone anyway, since we were trying to track down the rumors about an escaped leopard."

"But he only saved us because he was trying to save himself."

"What difference does that make? You have to judge him by what he did, not by his reasons for doing it."

"Well," said Nelson musingly, "I hope we see Wee Willie again. Do you think he'd remember us?"

"I doubt it, but who can tell? Cats don't talk, so who can ever say how much they know? I don't think I'd care to go into a cage with him, though."

"You know, Ted, I was talking with Mr. Holland while you were off looking at the chimps. I told him I liked animals, but asked him if he thought we should bother about animals, when there's so much other trouble in the world. You know what he said? He said that if people ever stopped caring about animals, the human race wouldn't be worth saving. He could be right about that, too."

www.ingramcontent.com/pod-product-compliance
Lightning Source LLC
Chambersburg PA
CBHW020658180626
46816CB00003B/1337